TO: QueeN

May abundance
BE your poretion
Bridgett
McGill

Redemption

Book 1 of the Sins of the City Series

Bridgett McGill

The Queen Within, LLC
Chicago, Illinois

Concept Development by Lissa Woodson: http://www.naleighnakai.com and

Editor: Marze' Scott: http://www.marzescott.com
Cover Designed by J.L Woodson: http://www.woodsoncreativestudio.com
Interior Designed by Lissa Woodson: http://www.naleighnakai.com

ISBN   978-1-7367830-1-6 (trade paperback)
ISBN   978-1-7367830-3-0 (eBook)

Redemption

Book 1 of the Sins of the City Series

Bridgett McGill

♦ DEDICATION ♦

To:
Zora Kartier Tillman
and
Makai Adewale Hart,
my children's children.
You are my Legacy.
There is an inheritance left for both of you.

♦ ACKNOWLEDGEMENTS ♦

My daughters:

Kwaan and Kayla – by biggest cheerleaders. I always believe I can do anything, because they believe in me.

Khaleelah Williams and Rainee Henderson who never let me lose sight of "The book they are waiting to read." Your encouragement has blessed me.

Naleighna Kai and Marze Scott, my editors, who were patient with me in the process and made sure to stop me when I needed to take a breath, so the end product could be excellent.

Thank you all,

Selah

Bridgett McGill

CHAPTER 1

The sound blasted into Ava's ears and sent the first-floor emergency room into total chaos.

Why is everyone screaming and running in slow motion?

She slowly turned in a circle, watching as nurses, doctors, and patients took cover under countertops, and others took cover behind desks, chairs, and gurneys.

Why are the police pointing their guns at me?

Ava's mind became clouded with visuals of every crime television show she could recall. Ones where innocent people paid the price for overzealous officers wielding guns with bullets that didn't have a direct target's name on them.

Why aren't they trying to find the shooter?

She tried to process everything.

Her mind and body were rolling through this scenario as though she'd become part of a black and white movie reel, frame by frame.

Why does my left hand feel so heavy?

Ava glanced down and the silver glint of the gun in her blood-stained hand twinkled as though signaling the only answer that mattered. She released her finger from the trigger. The gun took an eternity to travel from her hand to the bright white tiles.

The moment the metal clattered on the floor, the world became normal once again.

Ava could now hear everything clearly. Screams trailing into sobs. The woman barking orders through the overhead speaker.

Understanding was still a little slow in coming as an officer roughly grabbed her arms from both sides. In a simultaneous, quick motion, both male and female officers, each kicked one of her shins, pulling both feet from under her. She went down, her right cheek striking the cold floor. Pain shot up her head, and she saw stars, and not the kind that signaled a romantic night.

The burly male officer on her right jammed one of his knees into her back, while the female officer pulled her wrists together. The cold metal clicked into place and soon the tightness that bound them caused Ava to stiffen with fear.

What the hell just happened?

Ava cried, realizing that trying to explain to the police and triage clerk about the horrible experience that had transpired a few hours ago had fallen on deaf ears. Through uncontrollable sobs, the words came in a stilted fashion, recounting the details of what happened in that basement. Only three souls were there. Two of those were now damaged—body, mind, and soul. One she hoped was having a conversation with their maker.

Now she was on the floor, screaming with pain that kept shooting from her jaw to her brain. The portly officer's knee was digging into her side, all while cold metal restraints circled her wrists, tightening as she tried to break free.

"You're hurting me, get off me," Ava pleaded with the officer who held her down. Her rib cage bore the brunt of his weight, and his left hand pressed hard against her right shoulder as though she was still a threat somehow.

"Stop resisting," he commanded in the familiar words that proceeded the deaths of several innocent people. "You have the right to remain silent. Anything you say—"

"Get off me," she screamed. "What are you talking about? You're hurting me! I haven't done anything."

Tears blinded Ava because of the intense pain. She turned her head towards the officer, taking in deep breaths after he finally complied, only then was she able to relax her handcuffed wrists against her buttocks. She scanned the expectant faces of the patients and hospital staff looking back to her with wide-eyed curiosity. She searched for someone to help her, anyone who could explain why she had suddenly become the criminal instead of the man who had tried to do despicable things and believe he would get away with doing so.

She caught sight of a large pool of blood surrounding a man who was stretched out on the floor as if he was taking a nap in the middle of the frantic movements of those around them. Two emergency room attendants inched forward, then lifted him onto a gurney, trying to navigate the area without tracking the red sticky substance any further. A blonde nurse climbed on top of the body and pressed her stacked hands into the unmoving patient's chest in quick up and down motions. Another nurse moved a silver pole with a clear liquid IV attached. She managed to stick a needle in his arm, her steps perfectly timed to keep moving right alongside the medical transport. The head of the person on the gurney was turned in such a way that Ava couldn't see his face.

Ava closed her eyes against the salty, heavy tears that poured down unchecked because the handcuffs didn't give her the opportunity to wipe them away. The nurse shouted commands to the patient who was covered in so much blood there couldn't be any left in his body.

"Come on, stay with me," the nurse pleaded. "Can you hear me? Can you hear me? Come on people, speed it up. We've got to get this man to surgery STAT, we're losing him."

"Let's go, get up."

An officer on each side of Ava, pulled her up through the openings of her arms. She winced at the tightness of the handcuffs as their "assistance" was less than gentle.

"You have the right to remain silent," one officer declared, pushing Ava down the long hallway, speaking the terms that were familiar and ending with, "Do you understand these rights as they have been read to you?"

Everyone in the emergency room stared and pointed at Ava, those waiting to be seen and those who had seen too much. She shook her head, still trying to process what happened. Basement. Pain. Hospital. More Pain. Laughter. Rage.

"Do you understand?" the male officer repeated.

"Understand what?" Ava snapped. "Why am I handcuffed? What are you doing? I came because those bastards were getting ready to rape us." Then another thought swept through her mind.

Oh my God, where's Terri?

She scanned the area, which was now bustling with activity once again, in search of her friend.

The male officer jerked her arm again, harder this time. "I said, do you understand what I just said to you? Do you understand?"

Tears gave way to panic, with thoughts that she would feel this way for a long time.

"Miss, calm down," the female officer suggested above a whisper. "Just let my partner know you understand your rights."

The softness in the woman's voice created a small source of comfort. Ava angled her head, glaring at the female officer directly in the face "What's happening? What did I do? Where's Terri?"

The male officer nodded to his partner. They made Ava, who somehow became a perp, walk toward the sliding glass doors that lead to freedom for some, but was the beginning of hell for her.

A few steps in, Ava took in the large pool of blood on the floor, then flickered a gaze to the female officer. "Whose blood is that?" Ava inquired, panic lacing her voice. "Is it Terri's?"

"No, it's Alvin Murray's," snapped the male officer as he guided her forward. He leaned in close to her ear with a harsh whisper, "You might know him as Monty. Now keep moving, we need to get to the station." His voice raised two octaves louder.

Ava shook her head, her feet felt as though one hundred pounds had been added to them.

"No, No, No, this can't be right."

She quickly replayed the scene in her mind. The loud boom, then everyone ducking and taking cover. She blinked a couple of times, lowered her gaze, and the rest of the story unraveled with each step.

Penny's invitation. The party. The basement. His attempt to rape them. The blood. The pain. The handcuffs.

My God, what have I done? And where the hell did I get a gun?

CHAPTER 2

Khalil Benson lightly tapped both of his fists against the dark wood
conference table that fit perfectly with the etched wood décor.

At 6'3", he towered over most of the men in the office. His skin,
one hue lighter than ebony was always glistening because of his self-
care practices. His cheekbones and chin were sharply chiseled and
his teeth braces perfect; always giving way to a charming smile. His
slightly broad nose nestled between dark eyes, set under heavy brows.
Now that the winter months were approaching, he had begun to let his
seasonal beard grow, with a tapered goatee under a full bottom lip.

The crisp white shirt tightened over his muscular chest and a few of
the women at the table flickered an appreciative gaze his way.

"Bernie, you can't be serious man," Martin said, folding his hands
behind his head. "What's so important that we had to come into the
office on a Sunday? A *football* Sunday at that?" He leaned back and
rocked in the dark leather chair, a sure sign that he was beyond pissed.

The two female attorneys, Kara and Lisa, glanced at Martin and
laughed. Everyone knew he had money on this game, and they were

looking forward to his win. Especially since he brought lunch for the entire office from Ms. Libby's Soul Food Place and desserts from Old Fashioned Donuts the next day after the victory.

"Alright, alright. The sooner we jump in, the sooner we can get done." Bernie gave a nod to his secretary, Helen, and pointed to the projector. The middle-aged woman with mahogany skin and ill-fitting wig, flipped the lens and two headlines appeared on the screen.

Chicago college student shoots would-be rapist in summer bridge program.

Man dies three months after being shot by college bound, Chicago native, Ava Penwood.

"Looks like somebody did us an anonymous solid," Bernie said, tossing an opened FedEx package on the table, nodding toward Helen. She loaded a sheet of paper under the document camera.

"What we have here team, is a case of 'all kinds of bull'". Bernie continued, "Whoever sent this to us, wants us to do a little bit of leg work, but we have exactly what we need to reopen Ava Penwood's case."

The team of lawyers were now leaning on the table, attention fully focused on Bernie. Some of the women who were pushing fifty were focused for more reasons than one. Bernard Jefferson, a tall man with dark brown skin, was still quite the looker, if he—and the ladies—told the story. His short, gray tapered hair framed a square face, with a neatly trimmed goatee. Helen and Wilma, who was off today, were jockeying for marriage position, not realizing that Bernie was not aiming to replace his beloved wife in her earthly absence.

"Anyone want to take a stab at what we're looking at?" Bernie asked, scanning the expectant faces.

Lisa shifted in her chair, her smooth, peaches and cream face a mask of concern. "It looks like the page of a medical report."

"You are correct-a-mondo," Bernie said, grinning, while pointing an index finger her way. "Ms. Lisa, you hit the bonus round."

Khalil put his focus on the screen. "Whose medical report?"

"That's the question that starts the reopening of this case." Bernie slid another document over. "This is the medical report of Alvin 'Monty' Murray."

"The guy the college girl shot right?" Kara questioned, ignoring the impatient vibe running off Martin as she brushed a hand through her dark micro braids in the patch where some gold highlights had been added.

"Indeed," Bernie mumbled, taking a bite from his sandwich along with a few moments to savor it and give a satisfied sigh.

Martin Baskin, one of the litigation attorneys Khalil paired up with often, put his elbow on the table, and planted his face in one hand. "Bernie, you're killing us man, come on. Football. Sunday. Two words that are like gospel to me."

"Helen, let's see those pictures," Khalil said when Bernie's mouth didn't clear fast enough to give any instruction.

A stack of six photos sat on the credenza. Helen placed each one under the document camera. Photo after gruesome photo caused the attorneys to shift in their seats or frown with displeasure. Even Helen had to look away after a few of them.

"Those are some nasty-looking pics. It looks like someone had decayed body parts." Khalil said to Bernie, who evidently had a stronger constitution than the rest of the crew. He was still working on a fresh corned beef sandwich as though it was the first meal he'd had all week.

Khalil leaned forward peering at the last picture Helen slid in. "Is that a leg, or what used to be a leg?"

"You guys are on a roll today," Bernie said with his mouth full.

"Yeah, it's Sunday and we're hot." Martin's sarcasm was on full display. He took game day as serious as the criminal cases that crossed his desk. Thankfully his track record on winning cases were in tune with his game wins. Only Khalil has a better set of victories in the win column.

"Alright, alright," Bernie conceded with a pointed look at Khalil to bring the details home and shut Martin's grumpy antics down.

"So, it looks like someone at Cook County Hospital forged a page of the medical report in Alvin Murray's record." Khalil glanced at the page, then passed it over to Lisa, who did the same. "As you can see from the article, the hospital reported that Murray died as a result of the gunshot wound by Penwood." He moved an index finger, signaling for Helen to put the slide back a few images. "But someone in that hospital knew different and sent us this page and these photos.

"Get the hell out of here," Martin said, pounding his fist on the table. "So, it's another case of the Black Man dying in the hospital and nobody gives a f—."

"Hey, hold that down, brother," Khalil snapped.

"The prosecutor doesn't know we have these," Bernie added, swallowing a health drink to wash down a bite of his late lunch. "Our job is to find out how to get Ava Penwood's sentence reduced *or* have her out of jail altogether on time served. She's already been in three years on a thirty-five-year sentence for aggravated battery. That was bogus as hell anyways. That dude had damn near killed those two women with the quantity of GHB he slid into their drinks. Terri Brewer now resides in a rehab center right outside Chicago, still in a near vegetative state."

Khalil tapped the edge of the medical report, frowning at the words on the page. "The date rape drug, combined with the level of alcohol in her system sent her into a seizure. By the time the grandmother came downstairs and found them, she was almost dead."

"Yes, this is the kind of case we live for," Karen said with an appreciative nod. The firm had made a name for itself and a lot of enemies in the number of wrongful convictions they'd managed to have overturned.

The Innocence HUB was one of the first Black law firms in Chicago. Bernard Jefferson kept a promise to his late wife to staff mostly Black attorneys. He had opened the firm, known in the legal world as "The HUB", thirty years ago after witnessing an alarming number of Black people receive extensive jail sentences that didn't fit their crimes. His legal career started in the State's Attorney office where he found the disparity between criminals who had a lighter hue and European descent compared to those who looked more like the people currently sitting around his boardroom table, became too great to ignore. He vowed to spend the rest of his life helping people who became victims of a system where justice was blind to some and balanced for others.

This case, though, could shine a light on an already successful track record and put Khalil three years closer to becoming partner.

Cutting through the silence in the room, Lisa asked, "Alright, so what's our angle?" She tapped a manicured nail on the table. "She did shoot him."

"She has a point," Martin said, flipping through the trial transcript. "How much would the aggravated battery conviction have carried if he hadn't died?"

Khalil pushed the file to the side. "Probably fifteen instead of thirty-five, but we know how things really go. With a jury, those same elements—race and economic level—could work against her."

Kara extracted the pages from the folder in front of her. "From what I remember, she shot him at the hospital right after the attempted rape." She looked up a moment, her hazel eyes glazed a little, probably identifying with her own personal experience a few years prior. "From what I remember, the article said he tried to get away, leading the police on a high-speed chase. Then his dumb ass ran into a pole because he was driving under the influence."

"Then the idiot police took that fool into the same emergency room where the two victims were being treated." Khalil snatched up a sheet from the folder. "Evidently, he walked past her and started laughing, knowing he would get away with what he he'd done even in today's climate. She snatched the officer's gun and blasted him."

"Gangster." Martin's face had formed a "mean mug" and he was fully engaged, his mind mostly off football. Until halftime. Then all bets were off and he'd find a way to slide out to the breakroom.

"I remember" Khalil said, flipping to the next page, "People were siding with her on social media. If there was a case for temporary insanity ..."

"They wouldn't let her get off on that," Kara mused, and Martin held out his fist for a pound which she ignored. "I don't know where your hands have been." She shifted her gaze to Khalil. "White folks can get away with that, not us. Rarely, do we successfully navigate those kinds of cases."

No one disagreed with Kara's statement.

"Alright, that means I don't have to bring you guys up to speed, since our Ace seems to have everything well in hand before I even gave him the details." Bernie clapped a hand on Khalil's shoulders. "You're the lead."

"Did you just leave corned beef on my tailor-made suit?" Khalil, questioned Bernie with a sidelong glance at him then his shoulder.

"Even Poly and Esther can appreciate a little AP Deli," Bernie teased.

Everyone in the room laughed, knowing uptown Bernie had traveled all the way into the hood just for a sandwich.

"Kara, get all you can on Murray," Khalil directed, sliding the top page in the folder her way. "Lisa, find as much as you can on Penwood." He nodded toward the woman whose signature pixie haircut had been tried and failed by many, but looked amazing on her. "Right now, she's in Dwight Penitentiary for Women." He shifted a steely gaze to his mentor. "Bernie, I'm going to need you to use your community pull and find out who sent this envelope to us. It had to be somebody in the hospital who doesn't have anything to lose when the truth comes out."

Bernie paused with the last bite on its way to his mouth. "So, you're giving me marching orders now?"

"You said take the lead," Khalil countered, taking in Bernie's sour expression

"I meant for everyone else."

"Team player, Bernie," Khalil quipped. "Team player."

Bernie chuckled and put away the last of his meal and dabbing the corners of his mouth. He had always trusted Khalil with cases that brought good publicity to the firm, and with it more donations from people who had supported their pro bono efforts over the years. The minute the press found out that Khalil Benson had taken on another controversial case, Football Sundays would be the least of the staff's sacrifice. The wins were always worth it. Hell, they could buy their own lunch with those bonuses, but they also earned more notches on the conscious belt for every person they helped.

Bernie gathered the photos, medical reports, and other documents from Helen and tucked them all in a folder, before passing them to Khalil. "That's it for today. We can jump in tomorrow and go right to work, enjoy the rest of your Sunday."

Martin maneuvered around the boardroom table and skipped out in the direction of the breakroom—the halftime show was calling.

CHAPTER 3

"Penwood, you have a visitor. Let's go." said the stocky guard standing at the cell door with keys jingling on his hip.

Ava stiffened at the sound of her name. She was well aware that Ms. Dot was about to lay down every card in her hand to win the game. Two-hand solitaire was one of the many past times they had in their cells in the afternoons before dinner. Ms. Dot had a particular way of holding her mouth when she believed she had the upper hand and was about to smack down for a victory.

"I do?" Ava questioned the hefty guard, glancing up from a milk crate perched near the metal bunkbed. "I wonder who's here to see me."

Ava looked over to Ms. Dot as she stood and used a foot to move the crate closer to the wall. "My mama just came two weeks ago."

This must be urgent as visitors normally came in the morning.

"Girl, fix ya hair," Ms. Dot cautioned, giving her a toothy grin while stacking the cards into a pile. "Put some grease on your mouth. It might be a sexy man."

"Ms. Dot, you're funny," Ava said with a chuckle, then gave it a little thought. "But I will put a little shine on my lips. I don't know about that sexy man part, though."

Ava snatched a small container from under her bunk, dipped her middle finger in for a dime-sized portion. She rubbed the remaining gloss in her palms, then used it to smooth her dark, unruly hair. "Whoever it is, I don't want to be looking too rough. Might scare them off."

Ms. Dot gave a hearty laugh as Ava stepped to the bars and waited for the guard to turn the key.

The underlying stench of musk and bleach faded the second she stepped into the visiting room. A new scent wafted her way. Strong, but not too heavy. Manly, and not overpowering. Expensive for sure, and certainly nothing like the cheap Brut and Old Spice the guards wore in Dwight. Her gaze locked on perfection. Dark brown suit, broad shoulders and even with his pants almost covering the shoes, she could spot that spit-shine a mile off. He towered more than six feet, and commanded attention even before he parted those luscious lips to say a word.

Good Lord, who is this man right here?

Ava didn't say a word. Instead, she waited for him to look up from the document he was reviewing. With her right hand down to her side, her index finger slid up and down her thumb starting at her fingernail to just behind the knuckle. A nervous habit she still hadn't managed to break. Maybe Ms. Dot wasn't the only one who gave herself away with certain movements.

When he finally turned and locked gazes with her, Ava's breathing hitched. That deep, rich complexion covered a handsome face that was regal, smooth, and polished. He extended a hand with a braided gold band on his middle finger; she took note of the ring not being on his marriage finger. *As if walking down the aisle is anywhere in my future.*

His stealth presence alone was an outward sign that he had his life together. Ava's had fallen apart that one fateful night in Monty's basement. Every day she imagined if her choices had gone a different way—she refused the invitation, went to college, and right now she's an architect.

She accepted his hand as he said, "Hello, Ms. Penwood. My name is Khalil Benson. I'm here from the Innocence HUB in Chicago."

Ava heard only half of what he said and none of what it meant as she stared into his eyes, mesmerized by the smoothness of such a deep voice, and the intensity of his gaze. His strong, but gentle grip sent shivers through her body. *It might be a sexy man.* It looked like Ms. Dot knew something Ava didn't.

"Ms. Penwood?" Khalil repeated.

Ava blinked, breaking her gaze, finally releasing his hand. "I'm sorry, hello."

"Let's have a seat." He extended an arm to the steel bench as he waited for her to comply.

Ava eased onto the cold, hard seat as she admired the taste and fit of his garment. Pale yellow shirt, brown tie, red and beige houndstooth pattern.

"As I said, Ms. Penwood, I—"

"Ava," she asserted. "You can call me Ava."

"Alright, Ms. Ava," he shot back, smiling in a way that showed that he still wanted to keep a professional distance.

She smiled back and inhaled, realizing that this exchange was already the highlight of her day. Most days were filled with arguments, fights, making the best of the chow hall food, and long stretches of empty time.

"I'm here from the Innocence HUB." Khalil extracted a folder from a thin leather briefcase and placed it on the steel table. "We've recently received some information that sheds a different light on your case."

Ava placed both elbows on the table, bracing herself against the smidgen of hope those words and his presence pressed on her heart.

"What do you mean, a different light?" Ava inquired. "What kind of information?"

"I'm going to cut right to the chase because we don't have much time." Khalil flipped open the folder and extended a page her way. "It looks like Cook County Hospital may have been responsible for Alvin Murray's death. Meaning, he may have died from the hospital's negligence, and not the gunshot wound as they said when you were convicted."

In two blinks, her eyes went from being misted to salty, blinding tears. She wiped them away with the sleeve of the orange, cotton Department of Corrections shirt.

"So, what you're saying is my gunshot really didn't kill him?" Ava asked, her voice trembled as she fought to keep her emotions in check.

"That's what it looks like," he replied, flashing a smile. Ava could swear she heard a little song behind that one action. "We have some leg work to do, but the main piece of information is in our possession. In my remaining time here, I need you to tell me exactly what happened that night in the emergency room that led up to the shooting."

Ava inhaled, trying to process that first bit of information.

I didn't kill that man. All these years, she had been wracked with guilt. He may have deserved a bullet for what he'd done to her, but killing him was never her intent. Whether it was her plan or God's to send Monty to an early grave, Ava spent the last three years paying that hefty price.

"We have the transcripts of the case," Khalil said, placing a hand over hers. " I know it may be hard, but I really need you to take some deep breaths, close your eyes, and go back to that night in the hospital."

His instructions were slow and precise as he retrieved a yellow legal pad from the briefcase and a silver pen from inside that fashionable suit jacket.

"Why do you want me to close my eyes? "Ava asked.

Khalil shifted his gaze from the tablet to Ava. "The eyes are the organ that our bodies trust the most. So, even with them closed, they tell the body the most truth and that's what I need here. All of the truth, every single detail that you can recall, Ms. Ava."

Hearing Khalil call her Ms. Ava, made her smile again. She felt like he respected her the way she did Ms. Dot. To her, the title denoted how much she cared for the older woman and now Khalil esteemed her in that fashion.

Ava took a deep breath, inhaling the intoxicating scent of his cologne, once again giving her permission to close her eyes and relax her shoulders.

"Are you as comfortable as you can be right now?"

Ava enjoyed the resonance of his voice. Such a distraction. The same voice which had delivered the best news she'd had in a long while.

"Yes, I'm okay."

"Alright. You and Terri Brewer arrived at the hospital, and …"

She winced at the mention of Terri's name. A tear escaped, streaming down her cheek and a few others followed. When his hand covered hers, she exhaled, trying to center herself.

Many things happened while being in the belly of the Dwight penitentiary beast, and she had formed a mental shield to insulate herself. Now, he wanted her to let down those walls and relive the most horrific night of her life. She would have to if he was saying that freedom was on the other side.

"Keep breathing," Khalil commanded, almost whispering. "Continue taking those deep breaths. I'll be right here when you open your eyes."

She allowed herself to relax with the sound of his voice.

"Now, tell me what happened."

CHAPTER 4

"Ms. Dot, you won't believe what has happened."

"I'm listening, I'm listening," Ms. Dot responded, sitting up in her bunk.

Ava would sometimes refer to the elder woman as Mama Dot as their relationship grew to be more like a mother and daughter, especially after Ms. Dot's cancer diagnosis. Ava took the best care she could of her cellmate, and no one got in their way.

"You were right," Ava declared. "It was a sexy man. A tall, chocolate, good smelling, sharp dressed man."

She and Ms. Dot squealed with laughter; their hands cupped to their mouths like two schoolgirls.

"Not only was he mega fine, but he's also a lawyer from the Innocence HUB in Chicago." Ava handed Dot the card Khalil had given her. "He said his office had received some information that could prove the gunshot wasn't what killed that man. He's going to file a motion tomorrow."

Dot placed the card between praying hands that she lifted to her mouth, "Lord, you done blessed this baby girl for how she's been taking care of me." She rocked a little as though she heard some type of music that no one else could. "Won't he do it?"

Ava grasped the old woman's weathered hands. "I don't want to get too excited right now, because he said it might take a few months, maybe a year. His office is handling this case as pro-bono. He told me to just hold on. They're going to do everything they can to get me out of here on time served."

Ava moved away and tried to contain her excitement—she was almost skipping around the small cell. Ms. Dot, who could barely sit up from time to time, sat on the bed smiling, then eased back down on the two pillows stacked atop each other with her smile still in place. Probably the first real smile Ava had seen her have in a long while. She remembered the first time she and Ms. Dot laughed together in the cell; her first day in Dwight.

* * *

Smells that were too hard to separate caused a wave of nausea to hit as soon as Ava passed the threshold into House Two of Dwight Penitentiary for Women in Livingston County, Illinois. With no options to make a trip to the bathroom, she struggled to remain steady.

"Welcome to your new home here at Dwight, ladies."

The guard, whose footsteps were much faster than the trail of women following her, seemed to enjoy repeating the word welcome. Totally unnecessary because the moment those four-inch thick steel bars slammed shut sounded like a loud ass welcome all on its own.

"My name is Officer Peele. The man at the back of the line is Officer Mason. We're here to make sure you get to the exact cell that you've been assigned for your stay here."

"Move it ladies," Officer Mason commanded. "All of your new friends are waiting to get a good look at you."

Peele snickered as she gave each new inmate a head-to-toe once over and licked her lips at the ones who caught her attention. The dark brown bun just under the edge of her cap gave away the exact direction of her shifting gazes, and that ivory skin flushed with a little pinkish color when her focus lingered on the pretty blonde who struggled with the items she carried because she couldn't seem to stop scratching her arms.

Ava was glad to be moving after the three-hour bus-ride from the Cook County jail in Chicago. The ride was long, hot, loud and disgusting. At least three women were on their menstrual cycle and hadn't been given anything to take care of their personal hygiene.

After passing through the intake hallway, the sixteen inmates were divided into groups of fours.

"When I call your name, step up and form a line to the left. The first four of you will be going to tier two, Deck B, with me and Officer Mason," Officer Peele shouted above the loud conversations and other sounds swirling around the cell block.

"Queen-Esther Bell, step forward."

The pint-sized woman with doe eyes and a medium brown complexion, looked more like an eighth-grader than anyone's queen. As she sauntered past the guard like she was walking down the street on a hot summer day, she stopped and looked up into Officer Peele's round face.

"I go by Queenie, if you don't mind," she said in a sarcastic tone that made Officer Peele chuckle.

"Okay, Ms. Queenie," she said, then focused on the area they would need to move in. "Start the line to the left at the bottom of the stairs your Highness."

"Tina Marcel, step forward."

The skinny girl with stringy blonde hair and dull green eyes complied. She used her right hand to scratch her hair, then reached to scratch the inside of her elbow of the arm holding her blanket and pillow.

"Li'l ol' meth head," Mason scoffed from his place in the back of the line. "'Bout to have it real hard going through withdrawal." He shared a speaking glance with Officer Peele who nodded.

"Ava Penwood, step forward."

She gripped the blanket and pillow tight, then stepped over in the line to stand behind Tina, who was nervously shifting from one foot to the other and rolling her head in slow circles.

Peele gave Ava a hard glare before running her fingers across her nose, down to her lips and then cupped her chin. "This one here is real, real cute. Chocolate, natural hair like a young Pam Grier. Yeah, real nice-looking brown thang."

Ava gripped the pillow tighter as she watched the guard scrutinize every inch of her, lick those thin pink lips before going back to the list to call the last inmate.

"Betty-Jean Reid," Peele snapped and smiled even wider. "You know the drill, step the hell up. We see you have come back for another visit, hunh?" Peele laughed, rocking back on her heels.

Mason, cupped a hand next to the right side of his mouth, leaned in closer to Betty-Jean as he said, "You still getting yo' old ass locked up? Ain't you like, what, fifty-something years-old?"

Both guards broke into laughter. Betty-Jean gave them a stiff middle finger. "Whatever," she growled, moving past them to the end of the line while rolling her eyes at Mason.

"Alright girl scouts, let's move it, up the stairs," Peele shouted loud enough for her voice to bounce off the concrete walls of the place.

"I wonder why the hell she keeps yelling?" Queenie asked no one in particular.

"Shut it up and keep moving," Peele responded, clearly pissed off at being challenged by the tiny-bodied Queenie, who was totally unbothered by the officer's curt response. "Don't worry about how the hell I say something, just do what I say do."

After hiking up the twenty metal stairs, each woman stood in front of a cell in the same order they were called during intake—Queenie, Tina, Ava, Betty-Jean.

"Open Up," Mason yelled to the stocky male guard sitting in the command center. The click, roll, click, roll took an eternity before opening several cell doors simultaneously.

Using peripheral vision, Ava watched Tina start showing resistance to going into the cell. Tina dropped the pillow and blanket and was now digging and scratching into the same spot inside her elbow. Streaks of red blood streamed down her scarred arm.

"I can't, I can't," she cried, her voice trembling. "I can't kick in here, I'm not gonna make it. I'm gonna die in this cell, I can't go in there."

Tina backed away from the entrance. She shifted back and forth between her feet and started swinging her arms from side to side. Peele stepped from behind Queenie and stalked towards Tina, with a scowl that showed she was clearly pissed that Tina was holding up the process.

"Okay, you trailer park Meth head," she growled. "Get your ass in this cell. We have other business to take care of today and don't have time to be wasting on you." She tilted her head, glaring at the smaller woman. "I'm asking you nicely. Don't make me get ugly."

When Peele reached Tina's side, she tapped the bully club on the right side of her holster, squinting as the seconds passed.

Peele moved behind Tina and attempted to nudge her into the cell. Tina put both hands up and gripped each side of the entryway, planting her feet firmly outside the cell's metal threshold.

"I can't go in there," she screamed, and others on the block came out of their cells to bear witness to Tina's breakdown. "I need help. Please somebody, help me. Put me in a rehab deck, please."

Peele pushed harder in the center of Tina's back. Unfortunately, that small body held firm.

In one motion, Peele snatched Tina's left shoulder hard, turning her body to land a hard-right fisted blow to the stomach. Tina folded over and emptied the liquids in her stomach onto Peele's shiny boot.

"Oh hell, she's done it now," Mason mumbled and didn't bother to move forward to help.

"You nasty, trailer park trash slut," Peele roared, grabbing a handful of Tina's hair. She bent over so her face was even with Tina's. "I don't give a rat's ass if you live or die in here. Get your Raggedy-Ann looking ass in this cell, or your first week here in our lovely establishment is going to be seven days in the deepest pits of hell." Her shoulders reared back. "You wanna try to kick that two-hundred dollar a day meth habit you got with no methadone? You wanna try to get through that withdrawal that's gonna have you releasing your bowels every fifteen minutes with no help at all? Say. Another. Word."

She let those last three words drag off her tongue deep and slow. Tina winced from the lock of hair gripped tightly in Peele's hand. She managed to wipe her mouth, nodding.

Peele never released the grip on her hair as she pushed Tina hard enough to tumble and fall to the cell's floor, kicking the pillow and blanket in behind her as a way to get some of the vomit off her boot. She shook whatever remaining liquid she could from her shoe, then looked towards Officer Mason, Tina, and Queenie before shifting to the right to find Betty-Jean staring back at her.

"Anybody else got a problem with becoming part of the Dwight family? Just let me know." She adjusted the belt around a tiny waist, smoothing a hand down her hips and frowned at the remaining saliva on the black, shiny steel-toed boot.

The cell block was eerily quiet, awaiting someone who would be foolish enough to answer.

"I didn't think so," she snapped letting her gaze fall to the women in her line of sight. "Now the rest of you heifers step inside your new homes and I'm only going to say it one time."

Each inmate quickly complied.

An elderly salt-and-pepper-haired woman was stretched the full length of the bottom bunk bed encased in a thin metal frame. She continued to flip the cards in her solitaire game until she was asked to stand.

"Dang, y'all ain't even let the girl's body get cold before y'all done brought somebody else up in here," she complained.

Those words chilled Ava to the bone.

"I thought you said I was gon' have at least two weeks in here by myself." As she stood, she smoothed a youthful-looking ponytail over her shoulder while rolling her eyes at Peele who she towered over by at least a foot.

"I know, I know. I tried my best," Peele responded with raised hands. "But the powers that be wouldn't let it happen." She glanced at

Ava and smiled. "Anywho, this is pretty little Ava Penwood. Ava this is Ms. Dorothy Ann Wilson-Funches, known around these parts as Ms. Dot. You two will be cellmates for the next few years, unless a miracle happens."

Ava's gaze left the older woman and flickered to the stained mattress. The wrinkle in her forehead and lip to nose squint made Ms. Dot and Officer Peele laugh when Ava couldn't tear her eyes away from the sickening sight.

"Chile, that baby slit her wrist right here in this cell. Pretended like she was sick when it was time to go to the chow hall and did herself in."

Despair put a death grip on Ava's heart. Things could really get that bad?

Ms. Dot bent to reach under her bunk and pulled out a tote. After flipping over the top mattress, herself, she took the extra blanket, covered the mattress and directed Ava to put her sheet and blanket on top.

"Okay, Ms. Dot," Peele teased, grinning. "I see you trying to help a sister out."

Ms. Dot blushed and flicked her hand in the air. "Shut up, Peele."

"It seems like you two girls will get along just fine," Peele said glancing down at her shoes. "Now I gotta go finish my work before this shift change." She stepped out of the cell and gave a nod to Mason.

"Close up," Mason yelled back to the command center, then waited for the other guard to catch up. "We'll see who loses it first."

Their laughter echoed even after they made it down the stairs.

Chile, that baby slit her wrist right here in this cell.

Ms. Dot leaned against the top bunk. "Um, Ava, that's your name right?"

Ava nodded.

"I gotta ask you a question.

"Okay."

Ms. Dot peered at her a moment. "You ain't one of them butchy girls, is you? Because I ain't gon' rub on yo' booty and I shol' don't won't you rubbin' on mine. We cool?"

Ava burst out laughing. "No, I'm not a butchy girl and I certainly won't be rubbing on yo' old booty."

Ms. Dot gave Ava a toothy grin and winked.

Ava laughed and climbed onto the top bunk.

This was day one of her thirty-five-year sentence. How did an invitation to a party turn into the disruption of her life that she hadn't even began to live? If what she had just witnessed was going to be a daily occurrence, these days were going to be filled with chaos, sadness and drama. Would there ever come a time when someone would understand that she and Terri were the real victims and not Monty? She wouldn't let her mind sink into the dread of the time. Instead, she simply laid still and was grateful to finally be able to exhale.

* * *

Now three years later, the thought of an entire law firm fighting for her freedom gave her the hope she almost stopped feeling after the first year of being in Dwight. Finally, someone would understand that she was the injured party from that night.

At the trial, the prosecutor condemned her by portraying Monty as the victim, even though, he nearly poisoned Ava and Terri that night. Monty had given Terri a double dose of the GHB—almost enough to kill her. She was now in Skinner rehabilitation center unable to speak and barely alive.

Ava flipped Khalil's card over in her hand and realized one thing— she would finally have her day in court. She would have justice for herself and for Terri.

CHAPTER 5

"Hey London, what're you doing here?" Roman Beasley asked, scanning the rugged face of the man standing next to her, who definitely wasn't the man she was currently dating; his best friend "Where's Khalil?"

"What's up, Roman?" she said, trying to keep her expression neutral as a car whizzed past them in the parking lot of the Low Drop-In Motel a familiar spot for cheaters and prostitutes. "I'm dropping Neal off to surprise his girlfriend for their dating anniversary. Ain't that right, Neal?"

Neal Partee rubbed his index finger across his chin and his lips spread into a silly grin.

London could've smacked him upside the head, knowing damn well he knew who Roman was.

He must have felt she was ready to do him bodily harm because he finally said, "Yep, that's right. I'm about to surprise my girl with a ring." He tapped the bulge in his right front pants pocket.

She wanted to kick him. That bulge was no more a jewelry box than the hair on her head was bone straight from birth.

"So, why are you bringing him here?" Roman ventured, tilting his head and squaring his shoulders as though bracing for an unpleasant exchange. As a former police officer turned private investigator, his question had a tinge of interrogation.

Beyonce's song, "Friends" chimed on London's phone.

"Excuse me." London swiped her fingers across the screen and turned away from Roman's prying eyes to take the call. "Hey, girl. Yes, I'm here in the parking lot. I'm on my way up now." She tucked the phone into her bra, then faced Khalil's best friend. "We came in my car so his girl wouldn't see him. Now, she'll be totally surprised when she opens the door."

Roman's gray eyes narrowed on her as she tried to reel in her nervousness.

"You heard her call me," London protested, trying to keep an innocent face while tapping the phone inside her shirt. "She's expecting me right about now."

Roman didn't respond, but clicked the remote to unlock his car door.

"See you later, Roman," London added, using a hand motion. "Come on, Neal."

They maneuvered through the cars, the winding walkway, and up the stairs until reaching the third level. She could feel the heat of Roman's gaze on her, but refused to look over her shoulder to confirm his suspicions of her being at the hotel with a man other than her supposed-to-be boyfriend.

* * *

"Neal, don't call me again," London snapped, positioning herself so she faced the window. "You deliberately acted an entire ass just to cause problems."

"I don't know what you see in old boy anyway," he shot back. His raspy voice was once a source of pleasure, but was now so annoying she couldn't bear listening to it for long.

"It's not for you to see," she retorted. "We had an arrangement. You were supposed to keep everything low key and things would be fine.

You knew that was his boy and tried to make him suspicious on purpose. It's over. You messed this up. Not me. Lose. My. Number."

She disconnected the call and tossed the phone near her purse. All weekend, London had been waiting for that call from Khalil to pose his own set of questions about her whereabouts. Now, London sat at her desk at Clear Now Collection agency, in an office tucked between her girl Sadé and office hot boy, Tony. She couldn't stop thinking about the episode that could end the friendship that was finally moving into the direction of a committed relationship. London was unsure if Roman had mentioned anything to Khalil or if he was simply holding onto it for a minute. Roman didn't like London very much at all, so discrediting her would work in his favor.

She glanced at her phone and ignored yet another call from Neal.

"Damn, his boy *had* to be at the motel at the same time." She sighed, angling her computer screen so the Excel spreadsheet could be seen clearly. "Then made sure to call out my name so I would see him."

London had aimed to be a "guest" of the motel, preparing to have one last hurrah with Neal since she, unknown to him, had decided to fully focus on the relationship with Khalil. After all the games he'd been playing, Neal had given her all the excuses she needed. Khalil was certainly the better prospect as Neal had very little ambition unless it had to do with the bedroom. She was thankful for that phone call that came in from her girl Dominique right on time. Running into Roman had been too close for her comfort. Though she played the entire conversation off nicely, London could tell that Roman wasn't buying it. It didn't help that Neal wasn't playing along the way he should. His body language was giving off all kinds of wrong signals.

After hundreds of dollars invested in herself, years of womb healing, yoni steaming and wellness coaching, London was determined to not have the energy of two men in her body.

Neal was a boy toy with a limited purpose. Khalil was the real deal. Westside homeboy,

K-Town crazy, frat boy turned high profile lawyer living on north Lake Shore Drive. He was the best of both worlds. Cultured and refined, mixed with street edge. Smart, handsome, tall, muscular build. London had hit the lottery and hadn't even purchased a ticket. Women were throwing themselves at him faster than he could duck.

London leaned back and rested her shoulders against the chair's soft leather, then picked up the phone and selected "block" as another call from Neal came in. She couldn't believe the shift in her life after exchanging old habits for new ones and becoming part of the "woke" crowd. After giving up red meat and dairy, and practicing yoga, her body started changing, skin cleared and she was sleeping better. Her creativity flourished and artwork was selling. To top it off, she managed to attract a guy like Khalil. He had a great sense of humor and she was so grateful he wasn't stuck in that "broken wing syndrome." She'd encountered more than her share of men who blamed everyone else for things that had gone wrong in their lives. She'd had enough of the men who were unwilling to work through their own hurt and pain and instead, projected it onto others, especially the women they dated.

London was crazy about Khalil and wasn't about to let anything or anyone mess it up. She was still smoothing out her rough edges brought on by her tomboy nature. She was quite the rebel due to growing up with an overly critical mother; but now she understood that destiny was hers to control.

Khalil was worth every change she had made and so was she.

She smiled, glanced at the clock at the same moment her phone vibrated.

London never had to guess who was calling her at four in the afternoon every day, Monday through Friday. Khalil Benson never disappointed, ever.

"Hey baby," he crooned in a deep, melodious voice that made her melt. "How's your day going?"

"I'm good, I guess. No complaints," she answered, peering out the window facing the parking lot, noticing the empty spaces. Time had gotten away from her. "We haven't had too many customers today with the weekend coming up, but I've been busy enough for the day to pass."

London was always impressed by Khalil's ability to ask a question and listen attentively for the answer. He was unlike some men who listened strictly to respond.

"How's your day going, handsome?"

"I'm good," he responded, a shuffle of papers on the other end signaled that he was still at his desk. "Looking forward to the end of the day, so I can go home and relax. Hoping I can see you tonight. I have something pressing I need to discuss with you."

She sat up, bumping her knee on the slightly open drawer. Her heart slammed against her chest. Roman had talked with him.

"About what?" she hedged, closing her eyes against the pain that stabbed her heart as she thought of all the lies she'd have to tell just to keep him in her life. *Who are you going to believe, Roman or his lying eyes?* Classic line from an old television series.

"I want to bring you up to speed so you'll know what's about to happen in my life for the next few months or so."

London breathed a sigh of relief as the news didn't sound earth-shattering. "Okay, I hear you. I absolutely want to see you tonight. Are you coming to me or am I … coming to you?" She already knew the answer, but loved to hear him say it anyway.

"I'll come to you," Khalil said with a chuckle. "I don't want you out driving so late."

London twirled a strand of hair around her finger as she smiled. His concern for her always touched her heart. "What time? Seven, eight?"

"Seven sounds good, I have to go into the office tomorrow for this new case. I need to call it quits before midnight."

"Or you'll turn into a pumpkin," she teased.

"Prince Charming didn't have that kind of issue, but Khalil Benson is about to have a career-changing experience. This particular prince needs to be in top form."

"Okay, Love. See you tonight," she said in a soft tone. "Don't worry about picking up anything. I'm trying a new recipe. I think you might like."

"Sounds great, see you at seven."

London couldn't help but wonder what was about to take place in

Khalil's life that he was so pressed to discuss with her. Rarely did he bring the office home, which was one of the things she loved about him. Their time was all about them—not outside influences.

Khalil was the face of the Innocence HUB and the poster boy of high-profile cases. Normally, they would laugh, crack jokes or play games until the wee hours of the morning. London thought this case must be important for him to cut his time with her so short.

When he ended the call "Shoot, shoot, shoot" escaped her lips.

London was enjoying all of his attention being on her. They discussed their views on marriage and babies, bringing her closer to the point of a committed relationship with him. The last thing she wanted in their way was a public case that was going to consume him. She understood his level of commitment and his drive to win.

She slid into her coat, pulled her purse strap over her head and down across her body before walking to the elevator. London was frustrated at the fact that another high profile case could not only put a stall to her plans, but Roman could change her happy ending altogether.

CHAPTER 6

Khalil glared at his best friend since second grade, trying to absorb the information that Roman had shared.

"I don't know why you're always in the business of rescuing someone. Is she another one of your saving projects?

"No, she's not a project," Khalil protested, angered that he would take it to that level.

Khalil's gaze swept over his friend, taking in the seriousness of his facial expression. The freckled skin neatly twisted sandy locs and six-foot, medium built stature, so different from his own. They were often called salt-n-pepa. Even their homes were different. Khalil resided in a condo not far from Wrigleyville while Roman lived in a bungalow in the South Lawndale area, not too far from the police district where he once worked.

"Okay, she's not a project," Roman countered, leaning forward in his spot on the leather sofa, "but some of her behaviors have definitely been questionable."

The conversation between Khalil and Roman stretched on for fifteen minutes straight as Roman tried to make sense of what he witnessed.

Khalil gave London Tate the benefit of the doubt. They hadn't formed a happy medium.

"You can relax, you said what you said, and_I hear you." Khalil shrugged, shifting more comfortably in the recliner. "I wasn't there to confirm what you saw. So, how do I process it?"

"Okay, Mister hot-shot attorney. I see you're really into Ms. London," Roman taunted with a grin that was anything but kind. "And you're really feeling her. I'm just saying be careful. You know we go all the way back to the sand box, so if something shows up in your life that might have some stank on it, I have to say something. You know that." He glanced down shaking his pants pockets in search of his keys. "We're boys in every sense of the word and ain't no chick about to change that. I don't care how fly, beautiful, and woke she is." Standing, he slid into his mustard-colored jacket.

"I hear you," Khalil replied, leaning in with the palm-to-palm, chest-to-chest and hand-to-back shake up, reserved for deep brotherly love. Khalil opened the door and Roman stepped to the threshold. They both threw up an outward facing palm in true Que Frat boy style.

Khalil reclaimed his place on the oversized recliner, his long legs extending past the raised footrest. Roman's assertions were the worst thing that could come in his life right now. He was feeling London for more than a friendship. He hadn't been able to say the words before today. It wasn't just her shea-buttered, bronzed skin. She was so much more than the melanated goddess she presented to the world. She was authentic and conversed about living one's divine purpose. Adding to all that, Khalil had never met a woman who knew that *friend* was the true meaning of his name.

He really hoped she wasn't pushing to test his inner-gangster, because it would truly be a rude awakening for her.

Khalil didn't know what to think, but that conversation went to the left too fast for him not to believe that something was up.

London had his attention from the moment they met in a coffee shop across the street from the courthouse. No doubt there had been some questionable moments—strange phone calls, unexplained missed dates and now this. Dropping off some dude she'd never mentioned in a hotel parking lot to meet his girl? Roman's report made the situation harder to digest. Why wouldn't she have mentioned it to him? Having Roman come out with it first only added to any suspicion he would have.

Khalil was about to take on the biggest case of his career and needed complete focus. He would need Bernie's connections to push the paperwork up the wazoo to get the motion through. Before the conversation turned into everything London tonight, he asked Roman for help in tracking down the origin of that mysterious envelope. The man had been on the Chicago Police force for six years before hanging out his shingle as a private investigator. *He's been a damn good one, too.* Many of the cases from The HUB had turned on a dime with information he'd been able to collect. Roman's instincts were always spot on. His intuition was the only reason Khalil was even concerned that maybe London hadn't been on the up and up, and be on the out and out.

Khalil glanced at the files he had brought home from the office. Another woman needed his undivided attention—Ava's picture stared back at him with hopeful eyes.

He opened her file and began reading. Her height and weight were listed as 5'6, 126 pounds. He paused for a moment as he thought back to his first visit to see her in Dwight. As dingy and faded as the orange jumpsuit was it couldn't dim her natural beauty. Her skin, a flawless mocha brown. Her hair, wavy jet-black coils framed a soft lined face, with high cheek bones. Her medium brown eyes, accentuated her thin pointed nose. He chuckled looking at her eyebrows as he thought of his mother drawing her eyebrows on every day. Her voice was soft as she questioned him through slightly full lips. He closed the file and relaxed against the chair, ready to plan his strategy.

The prosecutor in this case had a formidable track record of his own. As much as Bernie believed this case was going to be quickly decided and dispatched, Khalil knew otherwise. Paul Jakes was angling to move up from the public defender's office to the Assistant State's Attorney seat. Not to mention the track of discord that was between

Redemption   41

them since law school. Winning the Ava Penwood case would give him
that leverage.

He poured a glass of Glenlivet Scotch from the familiar green
bottle, lit the Cuban Cohiba he retrieved from a gold-lettered engraved
humidor on the floor next to his chair. He pushed the recliner back as
far as it could go and watched the smoke billow into the air. Change
was coming. Hopefully everyone would still be standing when it was
all over.

CHAPTER 7

"London, come quick," Sadé yelled loud enough to reach London's cubicle. "We're in the break room, hurry up."

She pushed away all thoughts of Khalil and the regrets she had behind their last conversation regarding his latest case. She rushed from behind the desk, walked past the employee information center, until she made it to the room situated between office services and the bathrooms. A few other co-workers had left their stations and were right behind her.

"What?" London asked, frantically scanning for trouble. "What do you want? What's going on?"

"Girl," Sadé said, gesturing to the flat screen mounted on the wall between the coffee and vending machines. "Look atcha' man all on the news."

London turned to observe Khalil with at least six microphones pointed toward his face as he said, "With the evidence we have in our possession, we are working every day to have Ava Penwood's murder conviction overturned and her sentence reduced to time served."

Ava Penwood. The huge case London knew would be the end of their relationship, even though she knew she had messed things up before now. They still had a chance if he hadn't immersed himself in this woman's case. A relationship didn't stand a chance against The HUB and the cases they championed. That's why many of the lawyers were young, and single.

Khalil's voice was strong and confident in addressing the crowd. The reporters went crazy, throwing out question after question, pushing their microphones almost in his mouth. Khalil moved through the crowd with Martin in the lead and Big Rick, their security detail, pulling up the rear as they hurried into a black, shiny Cadillac waiting at the bottom of the stairs.

"So, you're dating a celebrity now?" Sadé asked, sipping a cup of green tea. She was a beautiful, tall brown skinned girl, who rocked shoulder length sister-locs. Because of her dangerous curves, she was known around the office as the Chocolate Jessica Rabbit. They had become great friends after she had been London's guide into her new "woke" lifestyle.

London stared at the screen, dazed as she filtered through events in her mind wondering how she could have done things differently. Khalil was about to take off and if she didn't get a handle on things, she'd be a thing of the past.

Sadé broke in, "You don't seem too stoked about seeing your guy on the afternoon news. What's up?"

London averted her gaze. "Nothing girl, I'm okay, it's just that—"

"Come to my desk for a minute," Sadé said, lowering her voice a little. "I forgot to do something before I came in here to eat."

Sadé put a plastic lid back on a container of brown rice and mushrooms and a mug on top. She sauntered to the door and waited until London walked past. Glancing over her shoulder towards the lunch table, she gave Paris a wink and big smile.

"I wasn't even about to let you start talking about your business with Ms. Holy Roller sitting there listening," Sadé said, navigating around the L-shaped cubicles that would take them the back way to the main part of the floor. "She was ready to get an earful. I saw her pen stop moving as soon as you said 'nothing.' I still remember her getting all bold at the Christmas party last year after she had a few drinks, telling us how much shade she had for us. What did she call us exactly? The witchcraft practicing duo?"

They laughed, turning into London's office space.

Sadé slid her lunch bowl in a brown paper bag while London sat in a chair next to the old wood panel desk.

"Alright come on and talk to me. Tell Big Sis what's going on."

"I'm so frustrated, Khalil told me at the beginning of this case he was going to need complete focus and it was going to become high profile pretty quickly. I've only seen him three times and talked to him briefly, maybe five or six times in the last few months. He said the case was going to get a lot of publicity, but I haven't been able to get in his space at all. He told me this was the biggest case of his career and there were discussions with his boss of becoming partner. I'm all for him succeeding, but damn, did it have to happen just as all his focus was finally on me."

Sade was rocking back and forth slightly grinning, hands on her knees, allowing London to finish.

London leaned forward in the chair and cupped her hands against her forehead. "We need tea and yoga. Or maybe wine and yoga. Or just wine."

Sadé laughed and said, "Can you come over to my house after work? You have some workout clothes you left last time. I washed them already and you know I have plenty of mats.

"What time are you leaving?" London's palms shifted until they were under her chin.

Sadé glanced at her watch. "Can you leave at four-thirty? Malik is coming over at nine. I'll send you home in an Uber at about eight. My treat, cool?"

"Oh, so kick me to the curb because the community peen shows up."

"I beg your pardon." Sadé narrowed her gaze. "My man is not community peen."

"Oh, you mean he's narrowed it down to a one block radius?"

Sadé glared at her, and for a moment London wondered about taking relationship advice from a woman who couldn't manage her own.

She stood and blew Sadé a kiss just as Ms. Holy Roller sauntered past and gave them both the side eye. London blew a kiss her way too, and the woman sped away.

They burst out laughing.

"Thanks so much, girl," London said, trying to contain the last chuckles, but inwardly one question had her mind in an uproar. Did Khalil have his mind on the case or was he avoiding her because of something Roman said?

CHAPTER 8

Khalil came to see Ava for two more visits. One, to let her know he finally obtained the motion, the next time was to prepare her for court. Months had gone by between the visits, as most of the fight happened on paper citing the finding of exculpatory evidence, but that didn't matter to Ava. The last visit with Khalil Benson had her smiling the entire day.

Even though Ava's sentence was thirty-five years and Ms. Dot had another ten years to go, they both agreed that forging ahead was better than looking at the bleakness of their current prison life.

The visits from Khalil that gave Ava the anticipation of her sentence being reduced by thirty-two years was becoming a reality. She clung to hope all those months and nothing could put a damper on things. Until the afternoon Ms. Dot came back to the cell with a sad expression on her face and threw a crumpled sheet of paper on her bunk. She plopped down on top of the two stacked crates, and put her head down and cried.

Ava climbed down from the top bunk, touching Ms. Dot's shoulder who pointed to the paper on the bed as an answer to the unspoken question. Picking up the sheet and reading it, she took a deep breath and squeezed Ms. Dot's hands in her own.

"That's what been paining my stomach so much, Ms. Dot confessed. It's why I can't use the bathroom and why I can't hold no food down. Damn liver cancer done got worse."

Ava did her best to hold back the sob in her throat. "Ms. Dot, we'll get through this. With all that you have come through, cancer doesn't have the power to take you out. You can and will beat it."

When the word "cancer" slipped past her lips, it sent a wave of emotion over Ava that she struggled to contain. Remembering her grandmother's valiant battle against the disease to which she eventually succumbed, opened a pit of despair in her belly.

Ms. Dot looked up into Ava's face. The tears made her dark brown freckles sparkle. She leaned over and wrapped her arms around Ava's waist and released the tears she had been holding since leaving the infirmary with the new medical report.

Ava didn't know how long Ms. Dot had been holding her, but the bottom of her shirt was soaking wet with her tears when she finally lifted her head.

"Look at how I done wet up your shirt." She sniffled, then used her own shirt to wipe the tears from her face. "I'm so sorry."

"It's alright, we're going to get through this." Ava tried to assure her as she rubbed the salt and pepper hair that was always pulled into a youthful-looking ponytail. Ms. Dot would always say she might *be* old, but she didn't have to *look* old.

Ava couldn't think of any more words to say to comfort Ms. Dot. She didn't know what would bring her any kind of solace in that moment. What she did know is Ms. Dot loved to hear Queenie sing.

Ava walked to the open cell door so the tears that now welled up in her own eyes wouldn't be seen by her cellmate. She glanced over her shoulder in time to see Dot stretch out on her bunk facing the wall. Ava peered across the deck, wiping her face with the back of her hand, then motioned for Queenie to come over.

Queenie walked up with the same devilish smile she wore that never gave away what she was truly thinking; until someone wanted to find out if her Napoleon sized heart matched the strength of her small stature.

"Are you okay?"

"Yeah, can you do me a favor?"

"What's in it for me?" Queenie was still smiling, but crossed her arms over a slight bosom and tilted her head back.

"I'll trade you three softies for a song for Ms. Dot."

Softies were a hot commodity in Dwight and other places where females were incarcerated. Personal hygiene products offered in state prisons were usually poor quality and provided minimal protection—the more a woman had, the better. It was common for the women to use cloth strips, notebook paper or whatever they could find during a cycle if they didn't have any sanitary napkins. Three softies were solid gold.

Ms. Dot turned to face them after hearing their conversation. She used her left arm as a pillow and closed her eyes.

"Bet, let me get 'em," Queenie agreed, glancing over Ava's shoulder to look at Ms. Dot. "What song do you wanna hear?"

Ava pulled three items from her tote under the foot end of Ms. Dot's bunk and handed them over.

"How about Angels Watching Over Me?" Ava asked.

"You got it." Queenie cleared her throat while stuffing the bulky pads inside the waist of her orange pants.

Ava stepped outside the cell, giving Queenie room to step in.

"I don't know what's going on Ms. Dot," Queenie said. "But for your girl to trade three softies for a song, is much love. This one's for you."

Queenie took a deep breath then belted out her soulful rendition of the old Baptist Church song. As her voice filled the tiny cell then bellowed throughout the area, soon every woman on the deck stopped what they were doing to listen.

The women loved to hear Queenie sing, especially at night or after a fight on the yard when tempers needed to cool. Ava always found it hard to believe a voice so big, strong, and beautiful resided in such a tiny frame. She truly had the voice of an angel that brought peace to the prison land.

When Queenie finished, almost every woman was filled with emotion. She hugged Ava and walked past her, her usual sly smile wasn't anywhere to be seen. The tears in her eyes said everything.

Ava stepped back into the cell and was greeted with a big hug from Ms. Dot, who kept repeating, "Thank you, baby. Thank you."

"It's alright Ms. Dot. You've taken such good care of me since I've been here. You stopped these guards from bothering me. You kept those "butchy women" up off me. And you even taught me how to cook Sunday dinner right here in our li'l cell."

They both laughed.

"It *will* be alright" she whispered, releasing the woman so there was a little space between them. "You'll see it's going to be just fine."

Ava couldn't have been more wrong.

CHAPTER 9

"Mr. Hinton, welcome to the HUB and thank you for coming down to meet with us." Khalil shook the older gentleman's hand and made room for Bernie to step up.

Bernie took Hinton's right hand in his and covered it with his left. The older gentlemen nodded to each other with unspoken respect and admiration. Khalil remained silent, allowing them their moment.

Bernie spoke first after releasing Hinton's hand. "We have prepared some refreshments for this meeting." He motioned Mr. Hinton to follow Khalil to the conference room that smelled of Lemongrass. Coffee, tea, water, danishes and muffins were situated on one end of the table. Each man selected pastry and a beverage, and took a seat.

Bernie and Khalil had already gone over what questions and answers were needed for the courtroom and which ones would stay in their conference room.

After they all had made it halfway through their delicacy of choice, Khalil began.

"First, Mr. Hinton, we greatly appreciate you sending us the information needed to re-open Ms. Penwood's case. We'd also like to thank you for coming today to prepare for court. We wanted to make sure you're ready and in the best position possible because of the media frenzy and the aftermath that's going to be set in motion after proving the County's negligence and cover-up in this case.

Mr. Hinton nodded and took a sip from his coffee.

"The prosecutor on this case," Bernie continued. "Paul Jakes comes from old, politically connected money, and he's gunning for a seat in the State's Attorney's office. He has great disdain for the HUB as well as a bitter history with our Mr. Benson here."

Hinton cleared his throat. "So, what you're saying is I need to be ready?"

"Yes, that's exactly what we're saying," Khalil chimed.

Bernie leaned forward on his elbows, interlacing his fingers, looking Hinton square in the face. "Khalil expressed to me the trials you dealt with while working at the County; thirty-five years' worth and you're finally ready to let it all go." Mr. Hinton nodded.

"I want you to relax and tell me in your own words why you sent this envelope to the HUB, why you waited so long and anything else you feel that you need to say at this time."

"Okay." Mr. Hinton nodded in agreement. Bernie continued, "We can discuss what we need to keep here and what we need to put in that courtroom. There is no judgment here. I am from the South as well and I understand and can relate to all the shit we had to deal with to become the men we are today." Turning to Khalil, Bernie kept talking. "Young Benson here has read about the struggles of the Black southerners coming North, but we both have lived it."

"You got that right. Thank you for saying that. I have been ready to say a lot, but have had to use caution, wisdom, and sometimes plain ol' silence to get me through life. Not just the thirty- five years at the hospital; no, it's much more than that. But for time's sake and this case, I'll keep it as brief as I can and stick to the matter at hand." Mr. Hinton had sat his cup down while speaking.

"Take your time." Bernie poured himself another cup of tea and sat back in the leather chair.

Hinton relaxed against his chair as well, planting his feet firmly against the commercial carpet and took a deep breath before speaking.

"I strongly believe that this case and what happened to that boy in the hospital has everything to do with Alvin Murray being a young Black man. He was unemployed, had no insurance, covered with tattoos, and smelled of alcohol and reefer when they brought him into the hospital. The staff paid that boy no attention, not even a simple workup was done on him. They just let him lay there, giving minimal care until nature took its course.

"Okay, how does this relate to this case, how can we use this to win, Mr. Hinton?' Khalil questioned. "I totally understand what you're saying, but the race card is the last one we would pull. We have to go with cold hard facts."

Bernie looked at Khalil and motioned with his hand for him to stand down. "Let Mr. Hinton say everything he needs to say before you ask a question."

"Continue Mr. Hinton." Bernie was speaking with a calmness Khalil had never witnessed.

"As a Black man who had served his country in the Vietnam war, a war I had nothing to do with as Black man, I came home and was still mistreated. As a decorated army veteran, I was treated the same way by Whites here as I was when I was a young boy in Mississippi on the farm, where my father was a sharecropper." Hinton laid a hand upon his chest. Bernie gave quiet applause to Mr. Hinton's statement, but didn't say a word.

"I was finally able to get a job because I was nice to the White people I served, who came to the diner for lunch every day from the hospital. When the medical records courier died, they needed someone to quickly fill the position. They chose me because I was a veteran with an army background. I was able to read and write, and was articulate. You know how they do, like they're doing us a favor, but they really need us."

"Hell yeah, I understand that. Happened all the time when I was in the states' attorney office." Bernie smacked the thick wooden table, as Mr. Hinton continued talking.

"As a Black man working in the County hospital, I experienced all kinds of discrimination from patients as well as the doctors and nurses I worked with. I saw Black patient after Black patient die because their needs were disregarded. This was the case with Mr. Murray. Hinton sighed a deep sigh and continued speaking.

"I'm not sure of the strategy you all are planning to take to shift this from the race issue, but this all comes down to the race card, if you want to know the truth." Khalil used a hand to cuff his mouth and looked towards the wall, past Mr. Hinton, who was still talking.

"The young man who lost his life is Black and so is the young woman you will be defending. The doctor treating Murray was Jewish and the medical examiner was White, so to answer your question, yes, hell yes, this is the hand that has been dealt, so the cards must be played." He took a sip of his beverage.

"I understand what you're saying Mr. Hinton, but we can't rely on the racism factor only. If you can start at the beginning and then we can figure out where to take it from there. Don't leave anything out, every detail is going to count." Bernie took a bite of his muffin and sat against the chair's back signaling for Mr. Hinton to begin.

"Okay" Hinton took another deep breath and explained in great detail how he came in contact with the photos, pulling Murray's file and his conversation with the Medical Examiner.

"Whew." Bernie chuckled as Hinton continued. "Dr. Mills told me he kept the hospital from being liable for Murray's death to the tune of $20,000. Weinstein not only had to pay Mills, but the funeral home director was paid to cover up the gangrene on the body so the family wouldn't see it. He used a hand to motion toward Khalil, turning to him at the same time.

"I was counting on Mr. Benson's wit to understand my note." Mr. Hinton nodded in Khalil's direction. He had left a simple message on a sticky note, on top of the medical record that read—Keep the numbers in order.

Khalil smiled and said "I didn't know what that meant, so I just started looking at anything with numbers. All the pictures, the medical report, the ID numbers of all the employees, but it wasn't clicking." "I went through every file for two days before I found it. At the bottom of the medical record sheet was a number."

Mr. Hinton smirked and nodded.

"It was so small I needed a magnifying glass to see them. I went through Murray's medical record. All the numbers were in sequential order until I made it to the sheet that recorded the cause of death. It was the correct form, but the numbers were out of order. I put the sheet I had from the envelope in order with the rest of the file and there it was, the numbers lined up.

Bernie smiled, nodding with approval the work Khalil had done. That partnership was looking more within his reach each day.

CHAPTER 10

"I've been sitting here twenty minutes and you haven't even gone back there to get him." Khalil recognized the screeching voice from where he sat, a short distance from the otherwise quiet lobby.

"Miss, I've already explained to you that Mr. Benson is in a scheduled appointment with a client."

"No, Ma'am," the voice contested. "What you're going to do is let me go to his office and I don't plan on waiting any longer."

Khalil pushed the comfy leather chair away from the conference table, moving a paper with a list of questions he used with Mr. Hinton in front of Bernie. "I stopped on question four, Bern."

Bernie rolled his eyes and shook his head as he picked up the sheet, angling his seat toward Mr. Hinton.

"How much longer is he going to be with this *scheduled appointment*?" London questioned in a sarcastic tone.

Heat built under his collar as Khalil approached Ms. Helen's desk, his irritation increasing as London's voice escalated with each word.

"Oh wait, would you look-a-here." London placed a manicured hand on the fullest part of her hip. "The man of the hour *finally* appears."

Khalil stood at the corner of the large oak desk and blew out a gust of air.

London quieted as her obnoxious antics came to a halt. She folded her arms and pursed her full lips—Khalil knew she was ready to grill him as if *she* were his legal opponent.

"I'll take care of this, Ms. Helen." Khalil nodded toward her, giving her a shy smile, which made the older woman smile in return. Turning his attention to London, and still speaking to Helen, he said, "My apologies for allowing anything to disturb your day, especially as it pertains to my business or present company. You know what to do."

"Thank you, Mr. Benson," Helen expressed as she picked up a coffee mug, glaring at London. "Please let this be the last time you have to explain to this young woman that this is not how we operate here." Helen stood, offering London a steely once over before walking down the hallway to refresh her coffee.

Khalil took another deep breath. "London, I don't know what the hell you think you're doing, but don't come to my job, getting loud and showing your ass. What's your prob—"

"My problem is," London snarled, her tone and volume remaining the same. "I've been calling and texting you for weeks now. You haven't had the courtesy to respond with a simple text."

"You're aware that I'm working, right?" Khalil narrowed his gaze on London's chestnut eyes and leaned in. "I gave you a heads up on what was about to go down. This is the biggest case of my career. I'm in a meeting right now with the only witness I have who can help win this case."

"For real, Khalil? Not even a short, 'I got you'?"

Focused on winning Ava's case, Khalil had managed periods of researching, eating, and sleeping, and not much else. The break from London followed the suspicious actions in the hotel that day, gave him an amount of peace he didn't know he needed. He wasn't considering breaking up with her, but the time apart gave him space to consider how she would fit into his world. London's loud and inappropriate interaction with Helen was enough for Khalil to make a decision. "You can't just show up here like this and act a fool. I'll call you as soon as I can."

"Don't stand here and patronize me," London snapped. "When a man wants a woman in his life no matter how busy he is, he'll make room. Keep it one hundred with me, Khalil. Do you want to move forward with me or not?"

"Do you really want to do this right here? Right now?" He motioned for her to step into an empty office to the left of the entryway and closed the door behind them. "People always say they want things to be kept *one-hundred*. But truth is, they're not ready for the one-hundred when it comes."

"Let's do the damn thang, Khalil." She put her purse on the table, folded her arms again, and dropped down into the nearest chair.

Khalil leaned with his back against the exit. "Look, you're an amazing woman. However, I didn't appreciate the several times you went missing on me at the beginning of our relationship. The longer we stay together, the more distance I feel between us. The hotel incident left a pretty sour taste in my mouth, and I mean very nasty." Khalil frowned as if tasting something bitter. "You said you were there to drop off a friend, but it wasn't a good look, London." Extracting a phone from a blazer pocket, he checked the time. "There's more I'd like to say, but not right now. Bernie and I are with a client, so I have to go."

"No, I came all the way down here to get this settled. You put everything before me, and I need answers."

"I will not do this with you," he said, releasing a weary sigh as she made things worse and proved a point she didn't realize she was making. "We'll get together and settle things when I'm done with this case."

He cracked the door, held up a hand motioning for security to come in the room.

Big Rick, opened the door and stepped in. "Right this way, Ms. London," he said, motioning an arm towards the door.

"Wow, you're gonna call security on me?" Tears glazed London's fiery glare as her gaze bounced between Khalil and the man who looked like a bouncer from an area club.

"I'll talk with you soon," Khalil assured, as London snatched her purse, following the directive given to her. "Rick is going to escort you to your car."

"I don't need an escort."

"I'll be in touch." Khalil started down the hall, heading back to the conference room.

"No worries, *Mr. Benson*," London taunted with a quiver in her voice. "You may be getting ready to lose more than just this case."

Khalil spun around in enough time to watch Big Rick lead London out of the building.

London's declaration was the nail in the coffin. Khalil hoped that she had no regrets. If she did, he wouldn't share in any of them.

CHAPTER 11

"The legal battle ensuing in the Ava Penwood case will be epic," one talk show host stated.   "Two of Chicago's up-and-coming attorneys contending in a case that will set them apart. One lawyer will become the new face of justice, and the other will forever be known as the loser in one of Chicago's highest profile cases,"

Being the president and founder of the HUB had its perks. Bernie had been made privy by an outside source who had been selected as the prosecuting attorney—Paul Jakes, nemesis to his star protégé, Khalil.

"Epic is an understatement," echoed another excited host. "In my down time, I like to go to the courthouse and watch the local lawyers in action. Jakes always gives Benson a run for his money. Every time they're in the courtroom together, there's a hung jury."

Khalil Benson and Paul Jakes had a rivalry dating back to their years at Johan Marshall law school.   Jakes always found himself in second place in most mock trials against Khalil back then. In his mind, Jakes was never much of a threat ... until now.

"How many trials have you witnessed between them?"

"Easily ten or so. Jakes comes for blood. Benson can poke a tunnel in a lot of his theories of a crime. Buzz on the street is Jakes is gonna win this case. It's supposed to be open and shut."

"Why retry the case after so long?" Whispered the petite woman as she shot a glance around the busy, tight space. "What's it been? Three years?"

"I hear her mother has been begging for someone to reopen the case because her daughter was innocent. But what mother wouldn't say that? There wasn't any proof that she was." The two employees shrugged. The man adjusted his tie and leaned into the coworker's ear. "But it was discovered that the defense has uncovered evidence *and* the presiding judge took an off-the-books bonus." With a tilt of his head, he leveled a knowing gaze, as the other staff member looked on in surprise. "I'll see you around. Keep your ear to the ground."

Khalil switched off the television. It was common knowledge at The HUB how determined Paul Jakes was to slam this case shut. Khalil knew every run-in with Jakes counted as a bruise to his ego and his position, whenever he lost a case. His competition always prepared for the next round, awaiting a comeback. The days of law school weren't so far away that Khalil forgot how Jakes's father publicly humiliated him and demoted him from a paralegal to a mere assistant because of his incompetence.

Khalil and Bernie discussed putting him as the lead attorney to ramp up and set the political stage. Bernie had groomed Khalil to not only be sharp, but cutthroat with a disarming smile. The training was from the time he hired him out of law school. Bernie never missed an opportunity to remind Khalil how he admired his drive and intelligence during the recruiting process. Plus, thanks to what happened with Khalil's brother he had the look, speech, and a personal vendetta with the justice system that would lend to his appetite to win a case. Khalil was on the way to becoming one of the youngest and most successful lawyers in the city, perfectly situated to take over the Hub if Bernie ever retired.

Not everyone in Chicago's legal world appreciated Khalil, Bernie, or the HUB. Their reputation for overturning cases had garnered more than a few enemies and Paul Jakes was definitely in that number. He had been gunning for the State's Attorney's Office since his first year in law school where the rivalry began. Jakes would be professional, but sometimes he didn't play above board when it came down to it. Khalil stayed within the boundaries of the law.

"We only have one day to get this done?" Khalil asked.

"One day," Bernie confirmed.

Khalil settled in the chair in front of Bernie's desk. "I don't know if I can pull this off in seven hours," he expressed, leveling a concerned gaze on his mentor and partner. "I know I could blow this out of the water with even just one more day, especially when I know that Jakes might get a little dirty. There's a reason he's so cocky. They know something we don't."

Bernie chuckled as he surveyed the conference room where three other attorneys sat alongside Khalil. "You ever heard of Johnny Cochran?"

"He's pretty legendary around these legal streets," Khalil answered as the corners of his lips turned up into a wide smile.

"I suggest you go watch a few of his more public trials and pull on *that* energy," Bernie advised as he shuffled a handful of documents and passed them to their clerk. "wouldn't have you as lead counsel if I thought for one second you couldn't handle this case. Even with all of our persistence, we were *graciously* granted a one-day trial. All other evidence has been submitted. They'll review it and represent. We have one witness and what is considered minimal, yet crucial evidence to be introduced - one day" Bernie extracted a folder from a satchel sitting on the floor beside him. "Word on the wind is that Jakes craves a promotion to the District Attorney's office. His last two cases brought him within inches of his goal, only to fall apart on the last day of both trials. We, more specifically *you*, Mr. Benson, will not be offering him any scraps. Make sure his dream dies on the courtroom floor."

The team was fully aware of the political engineering of this "save face" political act. The presiding judge had been removed from the bench and the one replacing him will be more fair. However, overturning this case against the state would be yet another David and Goliath's blow in Chicago's politically charged climate.

Khalil anticipated that this match could make or break The HUB's good name, and made up his mind that neither he, the team, nor Ava would be the meal that his enemy would feast on to accomplish that goal. The serpent was rising, and Khalil had to cut off the head, and free Ava at the same time.

Make sure that dream dies on the courtroom floor.

The entire HUB team discussed at length about the political can of worms that they prepared to present to the public with the newfound information that was discovered. One attorney spoke of plans to try a civil case on Ava's behalf for wrongful imprisonment. Another team member mentioned launching an investigation into similar cases, probing the medical examiner's records for Cook County Hospital in search for discrepancies in previous cases that could create a pathway to a class action lawsuit that would keep them busy for years to come.

Khalil had to bring his A-game—his career hung in the balance, but he couldn't leave Ava's life hanging there too.

CHAPTER 12

"This is a jury of my peers?" Ava whispered to Khalil.

The jury consisted of every type of citizen, except a young, Black woman like Ava. Khalil scanned the room; his pulse slowed a bit as his sight locked on Paul Jakes sneer from across the courtroom.

Breaking his focus away from his opponent, Khalil leveled a softer gaze on Ava and drew in a deep breath. He stood, straightened his blazer, gave her shoulder a reassuring pat, and sauntered toward the bench.

"Mr. Hinton, we first would like to acknowledge and thank you for your service to our country in the Vietnam War." Khalil placed the palms of his hands together and gave Mr. Hinton a slight bow.

Mr. Hinton nodded in return and absently touched the Vietnam war decoration on his lapel. The elderly gentlemen sat more erect, with his back against the witness seat. His low-cut gray hair and beard were trimmed with expert precision. He wore a crisp, white shirt under a black suit jacket— which made him look distinguished and proud. He gave the jury a sideways glance, then nodded to them as well. Some of them smiled. Inwardly Khalil thought *Good Job Mr. Hinton.*

"Mr. Hinton," Khalil asserted. "Can you please tell the court how long you worked for Cook County Hospital?" He stood next to the witness stand.

"Yes, sir. I worked for the County, thirty-five years before I retired."

"And what was your position for those thirty-five years?"

"I started as a medical records courier", he answered in a voice that carried across the courtroom. " Moved up to the clerk position, then to the lead clerk. I ended my career as the Medical Records manager. I retired a few months ago."

"We applaud you for such an amazing career." Khalil strutted over to the defendant's table. Martin took an envelope from a plastic bag marked *EXHIBIT A*. "Mr. Hinton do you recognize the information on this FedEx packaging?"

Mr. Hinton nodded. "I sent it to Mr. Bernard Jefferson, the founder of The Innocence HUB."

"And can you tell the courts what was in the envelope?"

Mr. Hinton shifted in the seat and cleared his throat. "Six photographs and the original page of the medical report on Alvin Murray. The original medical report on how Alvin Murray actually died."

"Objection," Jakes shouted as he stood to his feet. "Calls for conclusion of facts in evidence. Your Honor, the State does not have copies of these documents in question."

"Mr. Benson," the judge asked Khalil. "Was the state advised of the evidence you're presenting now?"

"Yes, your Honor," Khalil said, tapping the edge of the page. "We forwarded the medical report and photographs being presented today in question."

Jakes shuffled through a folder, then peered at Khalil, and shifted his glare to the judge. "Permission to approach the bench," he asked, sounding aggravated despite his cool demeanor.

"Approach," Judge Merrill huffed, already irritated before things got underway.

"Your Honor, the State has in its possession the medical record from the hospital stating the cause of death is a direct result from a gunshot wound. These six photographs and one sheet of a medical record are only copies," Jakes protested, as Khalil remained silent. "What does the witness mean about how the deceased *actually* died?"

"Let's find out. Step back." The judge waved them away from the bench. "Mr. Benson proceed." Judge Merrill folded his hands and relaxed against the chair as though this would entertain more than enlighten.

Returning to the defendant's table, Khalil retrieved a plastic bag labeled *Exhibit B*. He handed Mr. Hinton two sheets of paper.

"Mr. Hinton, can you take a look at these documents and tell the court what you see?"

The elderly gentleman held up both documents and examined them. He laid them on the surface in front of him and looked over to Khalil, who stood next to the table where Ava and Martin sat.

"If you're ready, Mr. Hinton, you may begin," Khalil stated.

"One of these documents is the original from the medical record of Alvin Murray. The other is a forgery."

"And how are you able to determine between the two?" Khalil asked as he turned on his heels to focus his attention on the jury.

Silence filled the courtroom, as the jurors glanced at each other, then at Mr. Hinton.

"Every page of a medical record is documented at the bottom in a particular way—page number, patient's identification number, the year the patient was in the hospital, and the medical examiner's credentials once the patient expires."

Khalil heard papers rustling behind him, an indication that Jakes was sifting through his files to verify those words.

"Mr. Hinton, again, please tell the court how is it that you can determine which of these documents isn't real?"

"Because in thirty-five years, there have only been two medical examiners," Mr. Hinton continued with a tone of caution. "Dr. Mills had been serving as the ME for the last thirty-two years. The fake form reads the patient ID number of Alvin Murray, ME ID number 058927 and page one." Mr. Hinton slid an index finger across the bottom of one of the sheets. "The original form reads patient ID number for Alvin Murry,

Dr. Mills actual ME ID number, 058729, page three.

Khalil pivoted and moved toward the witness stand. "Mr. Hinton, how can these numbers be so different?

"The numbers appear to be transposed, Mr. Benson. Everyone working in Medical Records must type their identification number *before* any information can be entered into a file. If there's an error in the identification number, the system flags an error, and the employee will not be able to move forward in their work. After three attempts, the system is locked to that employee, and it can only be unlocked by Human Resources."

"Why did those transposed numbers alert you?"

"I have a good memory. You learn the numbers of the only person able to sign off causes of death over thirty-five years. Also, every medical record file of an expired patient lists the cause of death on page *three*, not page *one*."

Questioning glances reflected through the jurors as they flipped pages in their yellow legal pads, adding more notes.

Khalil stood next to the jury box, but directed his words to Mr. Hinton. "For the record, there had to be an *intentional* transposing of the Medical Examiner's ID number, because the hospital system connects every employee to an ID number specific to each employee?"

Hinton shifted again, glancing at the jury.

"The original medical report shows Alvin Murray died because of gangrene infection stemming from complications controlling his diabetes. The alternate report was written to show Mr. Murray dying as a result of a gunshot wound."

The courtroom became much louder.

"So, Mr. Hinton, explain to the courts exactly what this means."

"That means that Cook County Hospital, was more than likely negligent, and responsible for the death of Alvin Murray."

"Objection." Jake hopped to his feet, face red, throwing his hands in the air with dramatic flair.

"Overruled, continue Mr. Hinton."

"According to his records, Alvin Murray didn't have any insurance, but what he did have was diabetes. The care for a non-insured patient is just a little bit different than the ones with fancy full coverage. There's no record of even a basic CBC blood work panel being requested that would have revealed his diabetes."

Khalil tried to hide his smile as he took a seat next to Ava and Martin. "No further questions Mr. Hinton."

CHAPTER 13

Khalil scanned the courtroom as Paul Jakes stood, glanced at this notebook, then back to Mr. Hinton. Jurors and those in the listening benches conversed in low tones.

"Mr. Hinton, you have a commendable background," Jakes began, giving Mr. Hinton a sly smile. "You served in the military, have been married thirty-one years, and kept one job for thirty-five years." His blue-eyed gaze slid to the jury. "One would have to question why you held onto such important information for so long, knowing that it could possibly change the fate of the defendant, Ava Penwood."

Mr. Hinton didn't respond, but the jury locked in on him.

Jakes stepped closer. "Mr. Hinton, do you have an answer?"

"You haven't asked a question," Mr. Hinton said in a sarcastic tone. "You made a statement."

Khalil turned to Martin and grinned.

"Alright, Mr. Hinton, noted." Jake's pale cheeks turned blush. "*Why*, did you hold onto such important information knowing it could possibly change the outcome for the defendant?"

Mr. Hinton shifted in the seat again and narrowed a steely glare on Jakes. "Mr. Jakes," he stated between gritted teeth, leaning on the bench. "I worked for the County hospital for thirty-five years. When *that* information came across my desk, I was three years from retirement. So, I did some investigation of my own. I found Alvin Murray's medical chart. The page that stated the cause of death had been replaced with the document that said he died from the gunshot wound. I asked around to find out where the envelope came from. A nurse told me an envelope was found by a mover who cleaned out Dr. Weinstein's office after he died in a skiing accident. He had the original with the pictures in his office.

"Why would the reputable doctor have transposed the numbers? What did he have to lose?"

"Staff that was intimate with Dr. Weinstein knew him to be prejudiced. Not necessarily against people of any particular ethnic background, but if you didn't have any insurance, he had no need to put his best foot forward.

The words were met with verbal whispers of disapproval.

"At any rate, if there is an examination of all the other fifteen thousand plus files in the hospital's medical records, you'll see all medical reports have the cause of death on page one and Dr. Mills' identification number is 058729."

Martin nudged Khalil, who shrugged at the fact that Jakes was helping to make the case in Ava's favor.

Mr. Hinton continued, leaning on the railing of the witness stand. "Later that week, I confronted the medical examiner who had taken the pictures. The examiner, Dr. Jed Mills, laughed in my face when I asked him about the forged documents and told me to mind my business. He told me that making waves so close to my retirement could be costly, so I let it be. At that time, my wife had to quit her job to take care of her mother. Losing my job wasn't an option, and I knew the day was going to come that I would expose Dr. Mills. I didn't know how much it was going to help the young lady." He gestured in Ava's direction. "I knew the time would come for me to reveal what I found."

Jakes glanced over his shoulder at the states' table. The woman gestured to the page in her hand. Jakes shook his head causing her to pull another page which he walked over to accept.

"Mr. Jakes, any further questions?" Judge Merrill asked.

Jakes held up a finger. "I do have a few more questions for Mr. Hinton, your honor. I know we're close to the lunch hour, so I'll make it quick." He ambled to the table, picked up another folder and handed Mr. Hinton a thin stack of papers.

"Mr. Hinton, do you recall the incidents recorded in these documents?"

The hairs on the back of Khalil's neck bristled—he had no idea what Jakes handed to his witness. A lot of nerve considering the accusation Jakes had tried to slide past the judge earlier, of Khalil putting in documents that had not gone through the discovery process.

Mr. Hinton's stony glare softened, and his shoulder slumped. "Yes, I am aware of what these documents say and I'm not proud of it."

"Could you please tell the court what these documents contain, sir?"

Mr. Hinton swallowed and flashed a sorrowful look at Khalil. "These are incidents reports."

"Were you involved in these incidents?"

"Yes," Mr. Hinton admitted. "I was in a physical altercation with Mr. Rooks, a former employee. The other incident was a situation with Mrs. Rashid."

"What was the outcome of these incidents?"

"I was given a write up for the incident with Rooks, and a suspension for the one with Mrs. Rashid."

"Both times by Dr. Mills. Why is that important?"

Heat rushed up Khalil's neck as he took a deep breath, and rested against the leather chair, trying to contain himself. Those incident reports had been sent to the Hub at the last minute. Martin had thought nothing would come of them. He was wrong.

"Mr. Hinton," Jakes emphasized. "Please explain to the courts why these incidents were followed by a write-up and suspension?"

"Relevance," Khalil asserted, leaning forward with both hands on the table.

Jakes spun toward the bench. "Permission to treat the witness as hostile?"

"On what grounds?" the Judge asked, flicking his wrist to look at the time.

"To show that Mr. Hinton and Dr. Mills have a history, in which Mr. Hinton has been waiting to get back at Dr. Mills."

"Dr. Mills nor Mr. Hinton is on trial here," Khalil asserted as he stepped in front of the defendant's table.

"Mr. Benson have a seat," the judge commanded. "Mr. Jakes, your request to treat the witness hostile is granted. Be sure it's related to this case, understood?"

Jakes nodded, the corners of his mouth lifting. "Mr. Hinton, who is John Rooks?"

"He was my subordinate."

"And what happened with the incident involving Mr. Rooks?"

"He came in to work one day exhibiting erratic behavior. He became a nuisance to the other employees. I advised him to take the rest of the day off, but he didn't want to miss a day of pay. Once he began kicking chairs and knocking things off the desks in my office, I handled him."

"Handled him? Hmmm." Jakes ambled toward the witness stand, snatched up the documents, and treaded the area by the rail in front of the jury. "Can you tell the courts about the incident that's described as an indiscretion between you and Mrs. Rashid? And before you answer, please explain why your shirt was open, belt unbuckled and her mouth was on your chest when your colleague walked in on you two in the breakroom."

"Objection," Khalil declared, trying to make sure the fury he felt did not come through. "Relevance, your Honor."

"Yes, I'd like to know that myself."

Jakes huffed and put his attention on Mr. Hinton. "Isn't this all just a plot for you to repay Dr. Mills for writing you up and suspending you for your indiscretion and excessive actions?"

"Objection, your honor." Khalil was on his feet, lowering his gaze down to Ava, who shifted her eyes to her lap, embarrassed for Mr. Hinton or possibly seeing her case being sidelined by issues that had nothing to do with what happened that night. "The prosecution is badgering the witness and twisting his testimony with details unrelated to the case."

"This has everything to do with this case," Jakes shouted across the courtroom as if the jury were a great distance from him. "This man is accusing one the highest-ranking medical examiners in this state of a hospital cover-up all because he wants to get back at him for writing him up for his ill-reputed behavior."

The judge removed his glasses, glancing at his watch. "Gentleman, this is not a shouting match, this is a court of law. Mr. Jakes, bring this to a close. Benson have a seat."

Jakes pivoted back to Hinton. "What do you have to say for yourself, Mr. Hinton? Isn't this really an attempt to get revenge on Dr. Mills? Do you really want the courts to believe this awarded Medical Examiner and award-winning hospital allowed someone to die in their care?"

"Mr. Jakes, I said what I said." Mr. Hinton straightened his stature, leaned forward, and tapped the railing. "Any write up on me will never overshadow the negligence that has been made by this hospital. Alvin Murray laid in that hospital bed in a coma, and did not receive proper medical attention. He didn't have any insurance, but what he did have was diabetes and nobody took the time to do all the proper blood work to catch it. When the body was taken to the morgue, the medical examiner took the pictures, prepped the body and put it back in the freezer for the funeral home to pick up. That medical examiner had been blackmailing doctors for more than twenty years and everybody in that hospital knew it."

Jakes threw his hands in the air with a loud sigh. "Objection. Your honor, the witness is presenting facts not admitted into evidence."

"Sustained, Mr. Hinton, please refrain from statements that are beyond the facts."

The room was in such a frenzy, the judge slammed the gavel at least six times and shouted, "Order in the court, order in the court." The noisy courtroom hushed.

Jakes' eyebrows drew in and his nostril flared at Mr. Hinton's carefully crafted deflection. Sauntering back to the table, he tucked away the evidence into a folder, an obvious attempt to gain his bearings. "I have no more questions for this witness, your Honor."

"Let's recess," Judge Merrill suggested, slamming the gavel before leaving the bench as if the seat had caught fire.

Ava and Martin stood, following Khalil's lead. The guard quickly detained Ava to escort her back to holding.

"I'll see you after lunch for the closing arguments," Khalil said to Ava, giving her a confident smile that she didn't return.

"Do you think everything is going to be okay?" she questioned, her voice small and wavering.

"Actually, I do," Khalil assured.

Ava returned a smile but it didn't reach her sad-looking eyes as he added, "I'll see you soon."

Khalil scanned the courtroom and met Ava's mother's worried eyes. His chest ached for any number of reasons. One, Bernie was sitting on the last bench in the room, next to Big Rick. Khalil couldn't read his expression. Two, the jury might not find Mr. Hinton as credible as he was before Jakes went in. Three, he made a promise to Ava, he wasn't sure he could keep with a jury that may be wavering. Jakes had drawn blood, and Khalil was wounded.

CHAPTER 14

The guard settled Ava next to Martin as recess came to an end and everyone filed into the courtroom. Her heart raced as Khalil was given the opportunity to redirect. He collected several glossy sheets of paper from the surface of the defendant's desk.

"Mr. Hinton, I'd like you to take a look at some photos of Allen Murray's body."

Mr. Hinton examined each image, one by one, back and front, making a pile as he stacked the photos. He laid the last one on the bench, then leveled a gaze on Jakes before shifting his sights to Khalil who had positioned himself next to Hinton, facing the jury.

"Are these the photos you sent to The Innocence HUB?" Khalil raised the photos one by one for the jury to observe. "The photos you're claiming Dr. Mills took of Alvin Murray's body?"

"I'm not certain." Mr. Hinton searched the courtroom as whispers from the audience reached the judge's ears and he held up the gavel.

"Mr. Hinton, *why* aren't you certain? You're accusing Dr. Mills of covering up medical negligence." `

"These photos are copies," Mr. Hinton asserted with a shrug.

"How do you know?" Khalil questioned, as he strutted across the courtroom ignoring Jakes' cocky glance. "You're claiming Cook County Hospital and Dr. Mills attempted a cover-up, and the photos of Alvin Murray were part of that cover-up."

Hinton released a heavy sigh. "Mr. Benson, I don't know where *these* photos came from because there are no identifying numbers on the back."

"What's the relevance of numbers being on the backs of the photos, Mr. Hinton?"

"All pictures taken in the morgue are captured with a special camera that automatically prints a serial number in the order the pictures are taken. The serial numbers and medical examiner's numbers are on back, so the photograph is not distorted in any way."

"Is that right, Mr. Hinton?" Khalil hedged with a pointed look at the jury.

"The pictures show how quickly the gangrene devoured his body in the time he laid in the coma."

Reactions from members of the jury ranged from wide eyes to dropped-open mouths.

"Bring those to me," Judge Merrill requested.

Khalil watched and waited for the judge's response—a deep wrinkle between his unkempt brows gave hope that it would work in Ava's favor.

Mr. Hinton relaxed in the seat and blew out a loud sigh.

The court room fell silent as the judge studied the photos back and front. Handing them to the bailiff, he instructed him to pass them to the jury. Further questions from Khalil only served to emphasize the point that the hospital was more negligent than Ava was guilty.

"Mr. Benson, is there anything further from the defense before closing arguments?"

"No, your honor," Khalil answered

"If you have nothing further to add, Mr. Hinton you may step down. Thank you."

Mr. Hinton, unbuttoned his jacket again and raised his hand to speak. "There is one thing I would like to say to you Mr. Benson, you Mr. Jakes, the jury and to you also Judge."

After turning from the judge, Mr. Hinton moved to the edge of his seat and began speaking.

"Today seems like the best time to clear myself of all secrets." Both attorneys stood, but Jakes spoke first.

"Mr. Hinton, are we now reaching for straws?" Khalil was silent; hairs on his neck again bristling. Mr. Hinton had already torpedoed the case. What else could he have to say.

"All of you lawyers think you do all your research and know everything." Khalil began tapping the table, hoping to send a signal that Mr. Hinton should pipe down.

"You, Mr. Jakes tried to use an incident report more than twenty-years old to shame me. Mrs. Rosalinda Rashid, is also Mrs. Rose Hinton. She was my wife then and she is my wife now."

Khalil dropped down in the chair, ignoring whatever Martin tried to whisper to him. The judge's eyebrows winged upward.

"The day Mrs. Rashid and I were accused of *indiscretion* was the Monday after we were married. She was a Muslim and her family disowned her for marrying me. She was at work crying because her family had refused to speak to her after we were married. That's why she was crying on my chest. She quit working at the hospital shortly afterwards so we could go on with our lives, she then shortened her first name and took on my last name, she has been Rose Hinton for the last thirty-one years.

The judge sat back with a smile on his face, interlacing his fingers over his belly.

"Mr. Benson, I ask again, do you have any further questions?"

For once in his life Khalil Benson had no words.

"No, no your honor, I don't. Mr. Hinton you may step down."

Mr. Hinton walked past the defense table and winked, with a big grin and took a seat.

The aroma of almond oil in the otherwise stale air wafted past Ava as Khalil returned to his seat next to Martin. Her mind raced with hopes of her release, while also not letting them get too high. Something about Khalil's walk from the bench made her believe she might be going home soon.

Voices in the courtroom murmured their thoughts loud enough for Khalil, Ava and Martin to hear. Grins were on the faces of Martin and Khalil. Even the judge seemed completely entertained.

Each attorney made his closing arguments—a wily grin slid across Jakes's face.

Khalil bowed his head as if speaking a silent prayer, and Ava joined him with her own.

Judge Merrill instructed the jury on their civic responsibilities, and each juror expressed their agreement.

"The jury is now dismissed. The defendant is to be escorted to the holding cell until a verdict is reached."

Judge Merrill slammed his gavel and left the bench.

"Boy, you did yo' thang up in here today," Martin crowed, patting Khalil on the back. "Your brother would be so proud of you. Hell, I'm proud of you. Ms. Penwood might actually get to go home."

Khalil turned to Martin and smiled at the memory of Ali. "Inshallah." He pointed an index finger to the ceiling.

Ava glanced over a shoulder at her mother who was sitting behind them, giving her a sheepish grin.

"Baby, everything is gonna work out," Vera encouraged, flashing a warm smile, but her lips trembled with emotion.

"Mrs. Penwood, we've done everything we can to make sure the jury understands Ava's innocence," Khalil said placing a hand over the older woman's trembling fingers. "Let's hope they don't take long to see things our way."

Khalil gave Ava a reassuring touch on the shoulder before she was escorted by the sheriffs to the holding cell.

Ava's heart pounded as she walked the lonely, narrowed hall to holding trying to remember what freedom felt like. Her mouth watered as she thought of her mother's fried chicken and macaroni and cheese. She wanted to smell the peonies in her mother's front garden; she wanted to see the view of Lake Michigan at sunset again.

Freedom suited Ava well and she was ready for it, but she couldn't help remembering that the jury seemed to warm up to Paul Jakes.

CHAPTER 15

"Ava Penwood," the guard shouted.

Ava surveyed the cell, and the women who occupied the space stared back at her. "Girl," one burly woman remarked. "You only been back here forty-five minutes. Either your lawyer did great, or he sucked. Good luck."

The woman laughed and several wished her well as Ava washed her hands and prepared to leave with the officer.

Ava used the last of the water to smooth any fly away hairs back into a ponytail—she felt Ms. Dot would approve. She paced to the door where the guard waited to turn the key. A second sheriff handcuffed her and escorted her back to the courtroom.

Khalil and Martin stood until the guard removed the cuffs, and Ava claimed a seat between them. Khalil placed a hand on top of hers, the same way he had the first time he visited her in Dwight. Ava's heartbeat took an uptick—something about his touch *this* time felt different, and almost electric.

Ava caught a glimpse of her mother's wan smile from her periphery. Heat crept up her neck and knots twisted in her stomach. She wasn't sure what this feeling was, but she hoped it was a feeling that she'd be able to get used to.

"All rise," the bailiff announced. "Court is now in session."

The courtroom witnesses, attorneys, and defendants stood, then followed Judge Merrill's example as he entered the room, took his seat, and faced the jury.

"Mr. Foreperson have you reached a verdict?"

The foreman who sported a bow tie and glasses stood, holding a folded piece of paper.

The bailiff retrieved the sheet and handed it to the judge, who reviewed the text and passed it back to the court officer.

"Mr. Foreperson, can you please read the verdict to the court?" The judge directed. "Will the defendant please stand."

Khalil, Ava, and Martin all stood together as if their moves had been choreographed. Khalil reached for Ava's hand. Ava bowed her head, dreading that the jury might say the word *guilty*.

"In the first charge, we the jury find the defendant, Ava Penwood, *not guilty* on the count of murder."

Ava lifted her head so fast her neck snapped.

The courtroom exploded with applause. Ava's mother screamed above the rest of the cheering crowd. Only then did it register.

Judge Merrill banged the gavel several times, ordering the courtroom to quiet down.

"You may continue, Mr. Foreperson."

"In the charge of aggravated battery, we the jury find, Ava Penwood, *guilty*. Ava's heart sank. The verdict was handed back to the judge and he instructed everyone to sit down. He sat for a moment, writing in a file. He looked up and asked the defendant to stand again.

"Ms. Penwood, it has been proven here today that you were not guilty for the death of Alvin Murray, but you were found guilty of aggravated battery."

Tears began to stream down Ava's face.

"There is no need to postpone and have you come back for sentencing."

"The 1,093 days you served at Dwight Penitentiary, before this court is considered your time served on the guilty count. Once you are processed out of Dwight Penitentiary, you are free to go."

Once again, the courtroom erupted in victorious joy.

Ava and Khalil embraced each other—she melted into the warmth of his strong arms, and her head fit perfectly under his chin.

Hot tears rolled down Ava's cheeks as she released the emotions that had been buried over the time she spent in Dwight.

Without speaking a word, Khalil pulled a clean handkerchief from the inside pocket in his suit jacket, and softly patted her face.

"Order in the court," Judge Merrill demanded.

Ava felt a chill as she stepped out of Khalil's hold to focus her attention on the twelve people who gave her a new life with two sentences.

"Thank you to the jury," Judge Merrill said. "Court is dismissed."

Khalil extended his arms in the direction of the guard, silently questioning if Ava would be allowed to hug her mother. The sheriff nodded and stepped away for a few feet. .

Martin patted Khalil on the back, and Ava ran to her mother.

Ava wrapped her slender arms around the full-figured woman who rocked her just a little unable to express her joy in words. "Mama, I get to come home."

"Yes, Lord," Vera whispered in her daughter's ear. "My baby is coming home."

Ava pulled away from Vera to see mascara-stained tears and wiped them with a bent finger. She turned to Khalil, taking in his handsome features—the fullness of his lips caused her to pause as she searched his face.

"Thank you so much, Mr. Benson," Ava expressed, drying the moisture that had collected under her chin. "You are truly heaven sent."

"I promised you I was going to do everything in my power to get you out. In twenty-four hours, I'll have fulfilled my part." He squeezed her shoulder and smiled.

Paul Jakes closed the distance between his team and the swing gate, leveling a grim glare on Khalil. "You think you did something, don't you, Benson?"

"No thinking needed." Khalil stated as he peered down at Jakes's short and frail-looking stature. "The jury said it all."

One corner of Jakes' thin lips lifted as his gaze bounced between Ava, Khalil, and Martin. "You think so, eh? We will see." Jakes blew past Khalil and stormed out of the courtroom followed by his staff.

The chill left behind with these words caused a shiver of unease to slither up Ava's spine.

"Thank you again," Ava declared as she gave Khalil one last hug. "I really can't thank you enough." Ava smiled bright as the guard guided her through the hallway to the bus to take her back to Dwight, only this time as a free woman.

Khalil and Martin packed away their documents and prepared to leave. "You ready for the frenzy that's waiting outside?" Martin asked with a grin. Khalil looked at Martin and to the back of the courtroom where Bernie sat waiting, while Big Rick stood next to the bench in the aisle.

Khalil's smile spread across his entire face.

"Let's do it."

CHAPTER 16

"Alright Ms. Ava, don't start me to cryin' up in here." Ms. Dot hugged Ava so tight she could feel the rapid heartbeat against her chest.

"You know if I start crying 'this cancer gonna' start actin' up and you aint' gonna be here to help me get through the pain."

Ms. Dot plopped on the bottom bunk, wiping her face with the back of a trembling hand. Ava picked up a duffle bag and a box and moved around the bunks to step out of the cell. She quickly turned back to Ms. Dot, bent over, and kissed her cheek.

"I love you, Ms. Dot. Thank you for everything." Holding back a painful moan that so badly wanted to escape her throat, she moved out of the cell before even more tears could fall.

Two days ago, she thought about how bittersweet it was going to be to finally go home. Being released from prison thirty-two years earlier than the original sentence was a blessing, and she couldn't help to be fearful of what was on the outside. She went to jail an eighteen-year-old, green-as-ever girl, who had just graduated high school. Now, she was leaving as a young woman, twenty-two years old, with no clue as to how her life would progress. She was done with the routines of the institution and ready to explore the opportunities life would bring.

"Let's go," said Officer Peele. "We've got to get through processing and it's gonna be a while."

"Okay," Ava responded, keeping her focus ahead so the other officer wouldn't witness her sorrow.

As she followed the guard with each step, the normal stale air became fresh air of hope to her, replacing the familiar smells she had grown accustomed to.

"Daughter," Ms. Dot yelled.

Ava turned to find a smiling Dot standing as tall as her frail body would allow. "Don't forget to let ya' self be blessed."

Ava couldn't believe a few days ago, she didn't have a chance of leaving prison. She ran back for one more hug despite the loud sigh from the officer. Ava left the prison a free woman her mind racing with bright ideas and wishes.

CHAPTER 17

Days since his courtroom victory Khalil finally had a break in his case load. He thought it was time to keep his promise of connection with London to discuss their relationship or lack thereof. Pulling a device from his pants pocket, he opened the screen and dialed her number.

"Hey, Khalil," London answered, her courtesy sounding restrained. "How are you?"

"I'm doing good," he responded, his tone was pleasant, but not flirty. The time for that was done. "How about you? How have you been?"

London paused as if she were trying to be strategic with her answer. "I'm well," she whispered, her voice deep switching to deep and sultry. "I've been looking forward to speaking with you. Congratulations on your case. I hear you did an amazing job."

"Thank you." Khalil cleared his throat as to not laugh at the way London expressed her desire for him through her tone. "Every one at the HUB put in hours of hard work as a team, and we won. It's our biggest case yet."

"I knew you were going to win," London said though she didn't sound elated, more resigned if anything. "You're an awesome attorney."

Khalil scanned the office that was now devoid of any photos of him and London. "Are you free this evening to have dinner? We still need to talk."

"I can always make time for you, Mr. Benson", she said and he was almost hard pressed to remember how she had come to his job and showed her entire ass. "Where and what time?"

"How about Provaré? We haven't been there in a while. I'll meet you there at seven."

Normally he would pick her up, but given the subject matter and the outcome, driving her own transportation was best.

"That works." London agreed, with a slight quiver to her response. "I'll be there."

"Alright, see you soon." Khalil's history with London had been rocky since the start, and the case with Ava added even more pressure. He knew that he'd have to make it abundantly clear that he and his feelings had moved on as London had become like a bad habit that never went away.

* * *

When London stepped into the entrance of the restaurant, Khalil greeted her with a friendly hug. Not a hair out of place and black liquid leggings that hugged every curve, and he noted that his body's normal reaction to her presence was non-existent.

"Hey handsome, I missed you."

"You look nice," he said upon releasing her.

"That's all?" London snapped; the corners of her red glossed lips turned downward. "I'm fine as hell every day of the week and all I get is 'you look nice'?"

"It's good to see you," Khalil replied.

Tears glazed London's eyes as though his compliment had hurt. His heart was pained as he had always tried to make her happy. The evening wasn't going to go according to what she wanted. "I think our table is ready." Khalil pointed to the maître d who signaled for them to follow him.

A low-playing jazz piano filled in the extended time when no words were being shared between them.

"So, you haven't missed me?" London asked, glancing over her shoulder as Khalil pulled out her chair.

He knew her well enough to know that she wasn't going to let it slide or mince words about the fact he didn't return the sentiment. He wasn't up for the drama that could possibly unfold, but he also wasn't going to be forced to say something that wasn't true.

"Honestly," Khalil said as he claimed the seat on the other side of the table of the dimly-lit corner. "I was focused on work and trying to win the case. My mind was on getting Ava out of jail."

London flinched as through he had struck her. "Oh, so now y'all on a first name basis? She's a *client*. Are you her lawyer or her friend?"

Khalil leveled a narrowed gaze on London, whose tawny complexion became more red as the conversation carried on. "You were working hard enough to get her freedom that now she's Ava and not just another client? For real, Khalil?"

Khalil's patience unraveled as London's voice became louder, and other patrons gave them curious glances.

"Alright," he said in a lowered tone, leaning in to speak. "What you're not gonna do is embarrass me. You don't need an audience for this conversation. Let's start over London."

"You damn straight," she snarled, decreasing her volume. "Starting over sounds good to me."

London snatched her black leather jacket off and hung it and her purse on the back of the chair. Leaning on the table with both elbows, and interlacing fingers under her chin, London looked as if she were preparing for a great debate of a personal kind. "So, let me ask you something, Khalil, and I want you to speak your whole truth."

Maybe a public place wasn't such a good idea. "I'm gonna always do that," he replied, trying to fast forward ahead in the process to navigate any emotion land mines. "What do you want to know?" London sat silent as if she were measuring her words. "I hope we don't have another incident like the one when you showed up at my office unannounced." Placing his palms together, fingers just below his lips, he leveled a steely gaze on London's fiery glare. "What's your question, London?"

"I've seen five or six news reports of you and this Ava standing next to each other and you two look ... more than friendly. My first question is what's the deal between you and her?"

"She *was* a client of the HUB, and I was her lawyer. That's it. Next question."

"Are you attracted to her?"

"London, you and I have been on and off so much, what we had could be qualified as a situation-ship, let alone a relationship. What makes you think I need to talk to you about who I may or may not be attracted to? All women have natural beauty and grace, unless they're snarling about business that isn't theirs and showing up in a professional setting and losing their entire minds. Next question."

London grimaced as though the answer made her nauseous.

Khalil knew his statement stung because he didn't single her out above the others. Declaring he didn't find Ava attractive would've been a lie. He tried to quickly think of what other questions she might have that she'd been holding onto. "Next question?"

London tilted her head and leaned in further. "Question three, have you spent time with Ava beyond any necessary court issues?"

"Hi, I'm Tricia," announced a middle-aged, brunette woman who places two menus on the table and prepared to take their order on a handheld device. "Can I start you off with drinks?"

"A glass of Glenlivet for him with water on the side," London answered. "I'll have a glass of Hennessy with cranberry. We'll be ready to order food when you come back with the drinks."

"Scratch the Glenlivet, please," he amended in a pleasant voice. "I'll have water with lime."

London huffed and slid back in the seat. "What the hell is up?"

"I'll be back with your drinks shortly." The server gave them both a curious look and hurried off.

Khalil picked up a menu and searched the contents. "Let me tell you something, London," he explained over the top of the cardstock. "This is over. *We* are done. Don't worry about me or what I'm doing. When I leave from this place, know that you are as free and single as any other woman in this beautiful city."

London pouted, her bottom lip dropped as the chipper waitress returned with their beverages. Immediately, she tossed the vessel of dark liquor down her throat, then plunked the glass down with a thud.

The waiter glanced at them both and offered a nervous grin. "Can I get you started wit-"

"No thank you," London snapped. "I'm not hungry."

Khalil glanced at Tricia and placed the menu on the table. "My apologies, but it seems we're cutting our evening short. May I have the check?"

Tricia tapped on her device and printed off a receipt, and Khalil reached into his pants pocket, paid cash for the bill and left a hefty tip for her troubles. Tricia grinned like she hit the lottery.

"Answer my question," London seethed.

Khalil stood saying, "Take care, London." Then spun on his heels and sauntered toward the restaurant entrance.

"It is not over," London screeched. "This isn't the last you'll be hearing from me."

Khalil continued to move until he reached his vehicle. London could be dramatic and sometimes theatrical, and based on that threat he had to prepare himself for almost anything.

CHAPTER 18

Martin and Roman burst through the door of Khalil's Lake Shore Drive condo, with cigars and whiskey in tow to celebrate his big win. Following close in step was Ms. Libby and the unmistakable aroma of some good old-fashioned soul food she no doubt prepared with one call from Roman—just what Khalil needed after the fiasco of an evening with London.

"Here, here, to Brother Benson, who has slain yet another justice system dragon." The three men stood and clinked their shot glasses together before downing their libations.

Moving to the dining room table, they found Ms. Libby had prepared a sumptuous spread. Martin rubbed his hands together, and Roman patted his empty stomach. Ms. Libby was their favorite small business to support.

"Alright, gentleman, enjoy." Ms. Libby smiled. "The caramel cake is on me."

Martin started pop-lock dancing like a teenager. "We got caramel cake," he sang. "We got caramel cake."

Ms. Libby doubled over with laughter, before giving Khalil a warm embrace. "Thanks so much for always supporting us."

"No problem, Ms. Libby," he said, hugging the robust woman. "Thank you for always making such good food and you know you don't have to bring those glass plates with you. I do have some of the good dinnerware."

"Son, I know that regular stuff is okay for you, but you're a man. A man that's making a difference in this world. You work hard, so you should play hard and eat good. The best eating happens on a glass plate where you can see through to the other side. Besides, it gives me a chance to see you when you bring the plates back. My daughter still has a little crush on you, you know." She winked with a big grin.

He smiled with admiration of the older woman, sliding the tip in her hand, and squeezing it gently and thanking his lucky stars that he had never taken her daughter up on her not-so-subtle offers. If things went sour, so would his ability to get some of this good food.

She squeezed back and whispered, "Thank you."

Khalil escorted her out of the door where her son and business partner waited. He washed his hands in the half bathroom next to the kitchen; Roman and Martin followed suit.

Jerk and baked chicken, jerk oxtails, candied yams, baked jalapeno macaroni and cheese, sauteed asparagus, corn bread muffins, a garden salad, and a pitcher of fresh squeezed lemonade, chock full of floating raspberries awaited. As each man handled portions that should've carried them into next year, no one uttered a word. Their unspoken rule – a man and his meal should be thoroughly enjoyed. Conversation would come later.

When the plates had been polished off, Khalil took them all to the kitchen sink and came back with three whiskey glasses.

"To my brothers in the struggle," he said in his best Jamaican accent, as each one filled their glass and raised it in salute.

"So, I wasn't there to see you in action," Roman said, taking a seat on the sectional and switching on some old school R&B. "But the news stories keep rolling. How in the hell did you figure out who sent those pictures to the Hub?" He grimaced as that amber liquid hit his throat.

Khalil took a sip of his beverage and held up an index finger while swallowing. "Because I'm a genius," he said with a chuckle. "That's all you knuckle heads need to remember."

"Okay dude, but how did you find who sent the information?" Roman pressed.

'I've got my ways," Khalil assured. Knowing it bothered his detective friend that he wasn't the one who came up with the goods this time. "All of them legal."

All three of the friends laughed out loud.

"Elementary, my dear Watson, it was simple calculation. One, I knew it came from somebody in that hospital. Two, it came from someone that wanted to remain anonymous. Three, I went back three years and subpoenaed employment records of everyone working in the County hospital from the time Alvin Murray was admitted after the shooting until the time he died, and I mean everybody down to the janitorial staff. Four, I subpoenaed a copy of Alvin Murray's complete medical record, and therein laid the path to success."

"Keep going." Roman was now sitting with this back against the couch after taking off his Kenneth Cole tan leather shoes. He was always able to get as comfortable as he wanted, Khalil's home, was his home.

Khalil sat on the edge of the couch, his eyes shining bright as he told the story.

"I'm getting there, hold on. Since the medical reports are kept in medical records, I started there. The receptionist was very friendly and more than obliged to answer a few questions. She made sure to stand up and lean forward, so I could get a good view of what she had under her tight-fitting shirt beneath her smock. I gave her one of my cards and explained I was researching a case. When she saw I was a lawyer, she opened up like the Red Sea during the great exodus."

"I started asking questions, like who was working there for the last three years that was currently employed. She said everybody had been there five years or more except the new Medical Records Manager, Patrenka Silas. She had only been there for six months. Then, I asked her, who was the manager before that and she gave me Hinton's name. She explained he had retired a few months ago. I made sure to leave an open door in case I struck out with Hinton and needed to start over. "

"That's my boy," Roman agreed. "He's been the set-up King since we were in second grade. Always, with the master plan." Their hearty laughter continued.

"Okay, so how did you get to Hinton? And how did you convince him to come to court?" Roman and Martin adjusted their positions to the edge of the couch as they appeared to be anxious to hear the good gossip – the winning kind.

"I made it back to the office and found Hinton's address and phone number on the web. I debated if I should call or just show up at his door. If I called, he had room to shut me down, then I would've lost the chance altogether. If I showed up at his house, I could plead my case before he shut the door in my face. With those options, the choice was easy. When I showed up at his door, he was in his yard trimming a rose bush and he tells me to come through the gate and that's pretty much all she wrote. He was still pissed at Weinstein and Mills and gave me all the information I needed."

Roman refreshed his drink and made himself comfortable on the couch again.

"Wow, that's really something how things transpired. It must have been her time to get out."

Khalil thought back to the zinger that could have made things end bad.

"Mr. Hinton didn't disclose the incidents that resulted in him getting written up by the doctor. Jakes pulled a fast one with that. It took everything to keep him from jumping off the witness stand and choking his ass. But the look on Jakes face on the redirect. Hinton is a feisty old man. The saving grace was when Judge Merrill asked to see the photographs of Murray's body, then passed the pictures to the jury. The diabetes had ravaged his body so much it was inexcusable. Those pictures and the fact Jakes got the incident wrong sank it for the prosecution."

"Luck was definitely on your side." Martin said, opening a bottled water and taking a swig.

"I have a lot of respect for the old man and all the injustices he's seen in thirty-five years, working in the hospital," Khalil said tapping the table with an index finger. "It wasn't hard to convince him to testify—he was ready."

"So, what's the girl Ava like?" Roman asked, refreshing his glass again. "She's not bad on the eyes at all. What's her personality like?"

Roman and Khalil went back to primary school and often Roman behaved like he hadn't left, at least not as far as his relationships went, which is why he was always up in Khalil's business.

"She's cool," Khalil said staring at the half-filled glass he held. "She got caught up in a case of the wrong place at the wrong time. No problems while she was in jail though. She shared a cell with an old lady who became like a mother to her. In the end she was the woman's caretaker since she was dying from cancer."

"Damn, talk about the good with the bad," Martin said over the rim of his glass. "She's definitely a looker."

"So what's up with London, How does she feel?"

"London is no longer a concern for you – or me."

"Wait, what?" Roman and Martin shared a glance.

"Ended things earlier tonight. That's why I called y'all, to celebrate two things at once. Ava's a free woman and I'm a free man."

"So maybe Ava is up next. I saw the way she looked at you."

"She's a former client," Khalil said as if he were defending Ava's virtue. "Whatever happens, I wish her well. That's it. That's all."

Khalil had caught himself thinking about her on more than a few occasions. He knew it wasn't a good look to pursue her, especially this soon after the case closed. "The HUB got the win, Ava Penwood is out of jail, and all is well. That's what matters," he declared as he shot knowing glances to each of his boys to shut that line of conversation down.

Roman and Martin glanced at each other, obviously wanting to say more, but keeping their thoughts to themselves.

"Alright, who's ready for some fun?" Khalil pulled the domino case from the bottom shelf of the coffee table. He shuffled the black and white tiles in the middle of the Oakwood table. "Let's slap some bones!"

Shaking away his thoughts of what happened earlier that evening and Ava, he selected his dominoes and organized them and his guests did the same, and looked forward to the distraction of his favorite game.

CHAPTER 19

"Squares, squares, loose and boxes. You need squares today, Ms. Lady?"

"No, I'm good." Ava watched the man wearing a camouflage jacket and wheat Timberland boots continue his hustle stroll and blend in with the Friday afternoon shoppers in the Jewel grocery store parking lot.

The chilly November wind was like an old friend welcoming Ava home to the Southside of Chicago. She scanned each corner and not much had changed in that part of the Windy City. Nothing compared to being back home and out of that six-by-twelve cell. Freedom was the most wonderful possession she had in that moment.

Ava tried to pull the short collar around her neck with her right hand and adjusted the duffle bag on her should with the other. It was stuffed to the zipper after combining everything from her box.

The moment she turned to walk to the store to get warm a deep voice behind her called out, "Miss Ava Penwood."

She turned to find the familiar face of Big Rick, from the Hub's security staff smiling. "Hi, I'm here to pick you up and take you home." He gestured towards a shiny black Escalade. She remembered him from her day in court sitting next to Bernie.

"Khalil sent you right?"

"Yes he did, Miss Penwood. Can I take your bag?" She handed the tall stocky gentleman her belongings and followed him to the truck. He opened the door for her and helped her step up into the vehicle.

The smell of leather and strong car freshener competed for the attention of her senses.

"Make yourself comfortable. There's an accident on the Dan Ryan, and we have a bit of a drive. We may have to take the streets most of the way.

Ava settled back and relaxed against the supple leather. "It's okay, as long as I'm on my way home.

"Let me know if you need me to stop and get you anything. There's waters and juices and a few snacks in the cooler on the floor. Help yourself."

Her stomach growled at the thought of food. The apple juice and honey roasted cashews were just what she needed to curb the hunger until she made it home. How sweet it was to even think of that word – home.

The trip to the Westside was made with only the sounds of an R&B station for company.

Ava tightened her plaited ponytail and smoothed the jacket as much as she could. She put Vaseline on her lips as Big Rick placed her bag on the porch and walked back to the vehicle. She inhaled the crisp air before ringing the doorbell.

A two-level brick bungalow took in the last signs of the garden straining to live under the coming frost. *Mama had always prided herself on keeping a well-manicured yard.* Ava thought of Mr. Childs with his extra loud lawn mower and wondered if he still came to cut the grass and trim the edges. The wind was strong, but the bed of multi-colored pansies were still standing and had expanded to the full length of the wrap around concrete porch. The five-and-a-half-foot steel fence was no longer red, but painted black—a nice contrast to the red stones in front of the pansy flower bed. Vera had updated the lawn furniture and the butt imprint on the pillow was evidence of Vera having sat through the summer watching the neighborhood kids play.

"Ava, baby," Vera called out from the front screen door. "What are you doing out here?"

Ava turned to find her mother's tear-stained face and outstretched arms, feeling the hug even before her mother reached her. The smile on her face warmed Ava's body like the July summertime Chi sun. "I'm out here thanking God for being on this side of the walls of Dwight."

Her mother's slow swinging hug was enough to release the tears Ava had been holding since the day she was informed that she was going home early.

Ava hugged her mother for what seemed like an eternity. She wanted to make up for the three years of being without the woman who loved and encouraged her during her time in lock up.

"Yes, God, thank you for sending my baby home." She whispered against Ava's ear. They tried they best to keep my baby locked up, but Lord, you had a different plan."

Ava gripped her mother's Sherpa housecoat until both of their shoulders were wet with tears.

"Mama, where's daddy?" Ava questioned pulling away from Vera's robe and glancing over her shoulder into the house. "I know he heard my voice, is he traveling or something?"

Vera gave Ava a reassuring pat on her back. "Come in and let's enjoy this food, I made your favorite meal."

Ava hung her jacket in the closet and moved from the front door into the transformed living room. "Wow Mama, everything looks brand new. What has gotten into you?""

Vera was moving towards the kitchen. "Mama's been doing the best she can. Thanks to that one lucky night at the boat. After giving Uncle Sam his cut, I was able to get the mortgage back down and do a few things I had always wanted to do."

"Well, you have done a good thing, it's beautiful in here. Mama, where's daddy?" Ava questioned again. "He hasn't even come to say hello since I walked in and now we're about to eat, he's not going to eat with us?"

"I'm gonna tell you everything," Vera said, smoothing a hand over Ava's cheek.

Something about the way she avoided the question put Ava on high alert. "Mama is something wrong with daddy?"

"Ain't nothing wrong that can't be made right." Vera closed her eyes for a moment as though sending up a prayer and worry crept into Ava's heart.

"I sure hope there's nothing seriously wrong with daddy. I don't need anything bad to be going on now that I'm finally home." Ava sighed, trying to keep her anxiety at bay. Prison had taken three years of her life. She hoped her time away hadn't stolen even more precious time with her father.

Ava attempted to continue the conversation with her mother.

"I have to say it again, the house looks really good, Mama what made you change everything?" Ava complimented as her gaze bounced from one area of her home to another.

"Thank you baby, so much has been going on, it's the one thing I had control over, so, I took advantage of it and made the best of it at the same time." Vera moved around the kitchen preparing for her and Ava to eat.

"Well, you just go girl," Ava teased. "You done moved all the way up." Ava stood in the front entrance of the kitchen, brushing aside thoughts of Khalil as the image of Ms. Dot came to mind. She crossed her arms to brace herself against the sadness.

Ava glanced over her shoulder. The dining room table was the same, but the chairs were different. *Mama probably found them at a thrift store or one of the discount outlets.* Being married to a man that ran a small mechanic shop meant being frugal when it came to finances. Instead of a simple plate and silverware, there were four place settings, including the placemats, chargers, dinner plates, salad plates and black ringed orange napkins to match were situated on the table.

Vera gave her a big grin and stretched her hand across the table after sitting down a bowl of cream style corn. "You like, you like?" She asked waving her free hand across the dining room table, like a Price is Right show girl, as Ava took a seat.

"Mama, I can't say it enough, the house is so pretty and so bright."

"Life is short and I just felt like I needed to start living a little bit more. You know, add some color to my world. So, hey, why not start in my home." Vera beamed.

"Say all that, Mama," Ava said with her right fist waving in the air above her head. Vera matched her movements. As a former Black Panther Party Member, waving a strong right fist always seemed to put her mother in a good mood and remind her of a time when justice for Black people were at the forefront of her life actions. Having a daughter caught up in the system was especially hard.

"Preach girl and get some color in your world."

Vera bent over laughing, placing a hand on the table to steady herself. As she finished with "Whew, my baby girl is still crazy. You always had your father's funny bone."

"Speaking of … What happened to daddy?"

* * *

"Hello, I'm here to see Eli Penwood." Ava handed her brand new piece of identification to the older woman at the front desk, her braided ponytail didn't move as she took the ID to record her visit in the guest register.

"Okay, Love, you're gonna go down the hall, to your left at the opening and he's the first door on the right."

Heat built up under Ava's coat collar, angry that her mother hadn't told her about her father's condition while she was away. After a stroke, he was rehabilitating in an assisted living facility, learning to walk and talk all over again. Vera explained that she didn't want her to worry about her father and just be more focused on doing what Khalil had asked so she could come home.

Ava didn't know what to expect when she saw her father. She remembered some of the women in Dwight having strokes and how damaging it was to their minds and bodies. Ms. Dot came to mind causing a sliver of pain to cross Ava's heart. The state exercised very little concern in their care of prisoners with cancer, strokes, or that they were elderly or infirmed. Most of them just ended up sitting in wheelchairs all day in front of the television, barely able to speak.

Eli Penwood's gray eyes lit up, tearing up as soon as Ava walked into the room. She wrapped her father in her arms as much as her arms could hold of him. She smiled when he returned a hug with equal measure of him.

"Look at you, Daddy." Ava pointed to the five-pound dumbbell her father had put on the floor when she came in. Wiping the moisture that ran under her eyes, "I see you're working hard. And you've got your motivation photo too." A five-by-seven photograph of her father in his Black Panther Party days sat on a nightstand. Her mother stood next to him with an afro that rivaled Angela's.

"Yeah, baby girl. I'm not trying to be in *here* forever," Eli said spinning a finger in a circle, meaning the facility. "You know how I am. I want to do things on my own. I don't want somebody helping me to go the bathroom and feeding me. None of that. I'm getting strong so I can come back home to your mother and to you." He picked up the dumbbell and started bicep curls proving his point.

Ava sat in the chair next to him looking around the room. "This is a nice room and it looks really comfortable."

"It's okay for now, but ain't nothing like being in the house we built. I really do miss sleeping in the bed next to ya' Mama, I can't wait to be laying next to my juicy girl again."

They both laughed at his nickname for her mother. Ava crossed her arms and admired the persistence of her father. His love for her was that warm supportive, compassionate respectful kind of love. He curled the dumbbell in one hand for five counts, then switched it to the other hand, repeating the exercise. She knew it wouldn't be long before her father had his wish, being spoiled by her mother. Their twenty-three-year marriage had been the example of the life she wanted to live, one of complete support for each other and individual endeavors as well as traveling the world to experience life together.

Ava caught her father peering up at her and then back down.

"What's on your mind Dad?" she asked, searching his glassy eyes. "I see you looking at me, what's up?"

"I prayed every day that you would be okay. You're my one and only baby. I've heard so many horror stories about young girls going to jail. You were only eighteen when you went in, even though you turned 19 two months later." Resting the dumbbell on his lap, he used the back of his hand to wipe away the lone tear that slid down his face. "I'm so proud of you for getting your associate's degree while you were in there. Education has always been important, that's how our people will get ahead in this world."

Ava sucked in a deep breath before she responded. "All those prayers from you and Mama worked. I had one cell mate for the whole three years, Ms. Dot. Everybody respected her, so nobody messed with me. It was a good thing I was in the cell with her because there were definitely some young girls in there that had it hard."

"You know baby, I ain't a church going man, but I'm thankful the Lord heard and answered my prayers." He pointed a curved finger toward the ceiling and she smiled as she gave the familiar tease that "You know the earth is spinning so you might want to point in the opposite direction." Her father laughed. "God knows what I mean."

After about thirty minutes of filling him in on some parts of life in Dwight, one of the young candy-stripers came in to let Eli know it was time for dinner. "Do you need help getting to the dining hall, Mr. Penwood?" the tall, thin girl asked.

"No, not today, my baby's here," he said with a proud lift of his chin. She's gonna help me."

Ava moved her father's walker in front of him, offering an arm so he could reach the apparatus.

"I get to go home next weekend for a visit." Eli shook some salt and pepper on his food and motioned for the hot sauce which she pushed across the table within his reach.

"That's cool. I'll be there, even with the new job, I can go home on the weekends if I want to."

"Okay, baby girl, we're about to dig into this food. They don't give us much time to eat before getting us back in our rooms."

Everyone at the table laughed with nods to that statement, of agreement, as they passed around the condiments in preparation to eat.

"Alright, daddy. I'll call you later this week to check on you. I love you." Ava gave Eli another kiss and before she turned to walk away gave one last wave that he returned with a food filled smile that made her day, as she turned the corner and headed back to the front desk to sign out.

Leaving the facility and moving past the pale walls and bland colored photos inside discolored frames she thought of Terri. She had learned she was in a facility, unable to speak and barely able to communicate. She wondered if she would ever develop the courage to go see her.

Ava's return home showed her that even though much is different, some things are pleasingly the same. Now, she had to shake things up in and get her life on a track where she could enjoy her newfound freedom. For a moment an image of Jakes came to mind and his threat to Khalil when he managed to free her. She wondered what Khalil was doing with his life. Who would he rescue next?" She secretly named him Superman.

CHAPTER 20

Vera dropped Ava off fifteen minutes before her starting time on her first day of work at Abigail House. The transitional home was located on the lower West Side, which was perfect for Ava and her family, who lived on the Northwest Side, about a twenty-five-minute drive away.

On the way to Abigail house, Mama went on and on about the spread she was going to have for Thanksgiving, Christmas and New Year's Eve. Ava was excited about the upcoming festivities. It had been three years since she saw any of her cousins, aunts or uncles. All of her grandparents had passed on, but getting together with the rest of the family was going to be such a treat.

The receptionist greeted Ava and directed her to the second floor to Sylvia Lumpkin's office.

"Come on in Ms. Ava, we've been expecting you." said a woman whose long gray locs were a beautiful contrast to her smooth ebony skin. She walked from behind a desk and gave Ava a warm hug. "I'm Dr. Lumpkin, but you can call me Sylvia. Welcome to Abigail House. You can have a seat here so we can chat a bit before you see your room."

"Okay, thanks." Ava settled in one of the comfortable highbacked, plush, orange chairs. Her eyes found the source of the sweet lavender coming from a diffuser at the end of the wrap around faded oak desk. Sylvia sat next to her in a matching chair.

"It's so good to finally meet you," Sylvia declared, giving her a quick once over taking in the casual pants suit Ava's mother had taken her to buy. "Mr. Benson spoke very highly of you and wanted to make sure you had everything you needed."

Ava smiled at the thought of Khalil making sure her accommodations were acceptable. She felt cared for by a man who wasn't her father. A man that made her heart skip and jump beats whenever she heard his name or he came to mind. She reflected on the first day he came to Dwight all the way through to the courtroom scenes. He had kept his promise from that first day.

Sylvia, handed Ava a manila folder containing several sheets of paper and a pen, with a clipboard underneath.

"Before I show you to your room, we need to review and complete these documents. Did you bring your identification?"

"Yes, I have it." Ava reached for a small purse inside her overnight bag that contained the bulk of her belongings. She refused to let her mother spend anything and let her know that any other clothes would come from her own paycheck.

The interview process and all the paperwork was completed within twenty minutes.

Although Ava had been in jail only three years, so much in the world had changed so rapidly. She needed to update her computer skills. Based on the description of her new job, she needed to learn the action plans set in place for the women in the house. There were a few more skills she needed to obtain.

Knowing the best way to assist the residents with their goals was important to her. She was grateful for the job so she wouldn't be a burden on her parents. She was even more grateful that Khalil had put in a good word to Sylvia and found a position for her as a staff member. She respected their concept of hiring people who had been incarcerated —the staff would relate to the residents' journeys, which could make the difference in their success in the program. Ava still planned to go to college, but her priority was getting on solid ground and this job was a great start.

"Okay, you have any questions before we go to your room?" Sylvia stood and put the folder with Ava's completed documents on her desk.

"No, I'm okay for now." Ava picked up her bag and followed Sylvia down the hall to the third door on the left. The brightness and feel of the sun's warmth filled the medium sized room and felt a bit like the new décor in the bedroom at her mother's home. After three years behind concrete walls and being allowed outside only a few hours a day, she was happy to have a window she could raise when she felt like getting some fresh air. The twin-sized bed, nightstand, dresser and chair gave the room a very homey feel; turquoise blue and pink paisley curtains matched the bed spread and pillowcase. The soft blue and pink tie-dyed flat and fitted sheets coordinated with the comforter perfectly. Someone had taste a lot like her mother.

"Be ready to have lunch at twelve in the dining area. I'll introduce you to the residents and staff. Today is Tuesday, so all of our outside vendors will be here conducting activities. You mentioned checking out the yoga class, so you'll be able to meet Mama Etu today as well."

Sylvia stood by the door, holding the knob. "Okay Ms. Ava, you can chill unless you have any questions? Ava shook her head. I'll leave you to get adjusted to your new room and I'll see you for lunch." She winked and closed the door.

Ava sat in the blue cloth chair and begin breathing in the air of her new space. "Thank you, God, for Khalil Benson. May God bless him and the Hub." she whispered as she enjoyed the view from the bedroom window.

CHAPTER 21

Khalil felt a slight dizziness come over him as Ava walked in the room, the corners of his mouth lifting faster than he could control.

"This is a different look," Ava said as she searched his form. "Brown Polo and khakis? Do you always look like a cover model? I mean even down to the shoes," Ava said with a chuckle.

"Hello, Ms. Ava," Khalil spoke as the corners of his mouth turned up. "Are you settling in?"

"I'm good," Ava said, her smile beaming. "I had a great time at home with my mom last night. I discussed my new position with Sylvia. Thank you, again, for the referral. I'm off to a great start thanks to the HUB." Ava averted her gaze from Khalil's eyes.

Khalil reached down to his side and placed a basket on the table wrapped in cellophane, tied with a shimmery silver bow.

"Everybody at the Innocence HUB wanted to make sure you have everything you need," Khalil explained. "The ladies took that opportunity to go on a shopping spree. There's lotion, Vaseline, body wash, sponges, hair products, shea butter, some oils, pencils, pens, feminine products, a comb and brush, and gift cards to Walmart and Jewel. The gray envelope is from me."

"Wow, this is beautiful, and I do need everything in here." Ava kept looking at the basket and shuffled through the items as Khalil held the basket. "Please tell everyone I'm so grateful. I appreciate you taking the time to come see me and bring this gift."

"Will do and it's no problem at all." Khalil reached into a pocket, extracted a wallet-sized billfold, and handed Ava a business card. "Let me know if there's anything you require. I'll make sure you get ... whatever you need."

Ava reached to retrieve the basket, and the slight touch of her hand sent chills up Khalil's arm. Breaking the momentary silence, Khalil announced, "I suppose I'll go now. Enjoy the contents of the basket. The ladies will be glad to know you liked it."

The receptionist, Margo Blanks, grinned as she tapped a pencil against the surface of the table in front of her. "Nice that you're making sure she's good, Mr. Benson."

"I think she deserves it," Khalil expressed, steadying his gaze on Ava.

An exquisite blush spread across Ava's cheeks, adding to her natural beauty. Khalil stepped back to the reception desk and extended an arm, signaling for her to leave out first.

Ava blushed as she adjusted the basket in her arms, and Khalil was surprised that he couldn't control the heat rising to the nape of his neck. An awkward moment of silence hung between them as they stood in the foyer like smitten teenagers.

"Thank you for getting me this job," Ava said, breaking the silence this time around.

"No worries," Khalil returned, his heart pumping faster with every word he spoke. "Getting back on your feet is of the utmost importance."

"True," Ava agreed, taking a step back as if she were preparing to leave. "Once I'm settled, I'll be enrolling in school. My dream is delayed, but not deferred."

Khalil reached to take the basket out of Ava's hand. "What are you doing?" Ava asked with a chuckle.

"May I give you a hug?" Khalil asked, holding his arms open. "I'm so proud of you. A celebratory hug is in order."

Ava's eyes lit up as he placed the basket on the floor and leaned into Khalil's body.

Khalil wrapped his strapping arms around Ava and chose not to squeeze her despite his desire. She felt so good, like she was a perfect fit to his body and soul. He had never experienced this feeling with London.

Releasing her from his embrace, a chill raced through Khalil's body as he missed her warmth. "Alright then, I'll check on you next week."

"I look forward to hearing from you." Ava gleamed, turning on her heals and walking down the hall.

Khalil watched Ava amble down the corridor, a smile splitting his face as he noticed a bounce to her step. Thoughts paced through his mind, knowing he wanted to establish more than a business relationship, however not confident it was the best idea since Ava might still be seen as a client of the HUB.

Entering through the front doors of Abigail House, he was dropping off a gift of a fresh start. Leaving out, he wanted a new beginning with the woman he yearned for. As he strutted to the parking lot, he knew a decision would need to be made. What he didn't know was how Ava felt. At this point, the prayers he had for a positive outcome for the trial will now be put to good use in winning Ava's heart.

CHAPTER 22

The handwriting was perfect cursive and so neat, Ava wondered if Khalil had written it himself. Ava laid against the pillow. Inhaling the intoxicating scent from the card, Ava held the note with both hands against her chest.

"Thank you, Mr. Benson, with your fine self," Ava said to herself. She left the card he sent her for graduation while in Dwight in her bedroom closet at home. Now, she has another message from him. She loved the idea of being reminded of him in both places. She wondered if he would ever look at her as more than a client.

A smile spread from one side of her face to the other as she thought back to last the card he sent to her back in Dwight. She could still hear Ms. Dot's voice.

"This man done sent you this beautiful card and $200. Girl, please, that man is liking on you." Ms. Dot nodded, grinning from ear to ear.

"Ms. Dot, he probably just sent this money on behalf of the law firm, they're probably going to write it off on their taxes." Ava blushed, still surprised by Khalil's gesture.

"Okay, keep on thinking that. You can buy all the sanitary napkins, zoos zoos and whams whams you want with $200." Ms. Dot was standing with one hand on her hip and the other hand pointing an index finger towards Ava.

They both laughed hysterically.

Ava removed the card from the envelope and sat it on the nightstand. She sat up and placed her feet on the floor. As she traced the butterfly on the front of the card with her index finger, she remembered the moment she decided to stop counting herself out.

In the first ten months in Dwight, Ava saw so many inmates give up hope. She promised herself that if the prison system took away everything, she would never allow her most important commodity to be stolen—she would never lose hope.

With two special cards from Khalil, hope was still holding its position in her space

"I am living in my present; my past cannot hold me back and my future is waiting for me. I'm as worthy as any other woman to be chosen by such a special man." These became her daily affirmations. She had developed feelings for him during his visits to Dwight. She decided if Khalil wasn't in her future, at least she knew what it would look like to have a man who protected her by word and deed.

She wanted to get comfortable early and do some reading. She ambled down the hall to the resident bathroom, which smelled of the same lavender in Sylvia's office.

After showering, she went to the kitchen in search of hot water. A purple mug with the words YOU GOT THIS written in black cursive across the cup and a box of chamomile tea were inside the basket. She had heard somewhere that it was good for relaxation and sleeping.

A sudden noise behind her nearly caused the mug to slip from her hands.

A pint-sized woman with big eyes and the complexion of honey stood in the doorway.

"I see we got somebody new around here." She leaned against the entrance with her arms crossed over her bosom. "I'm Zola."

"I'm Ava—Ava Penwood." She steeped the tea bag in the cup, out of her peripheral vision, she could see that Zola was sizing her up. She took a mental note to find out more about Ms. Zola. Habits formed in prison don't die easily.

For her first week, she would participate in the same activities as the residents in order to better service them. Ava attended the yoga class on her second day at Abigail House. Mama Etu was known as the Holistic Healer Yoga Instructor. The women in the yoga class put her at more ease than Zola.

"Ava, I'd like to speak with you after class," Mama Etu requested.

"Sure thing." Ava agreed.

Once class was over, Mama Etu rolled up her mat, folded her towel, and walked over to a set of cabinets by Ava. "Khalil Benson wanted me to take a minute and speak with you so I can understand exactly what your needs are," she stated as she slid the yoga mat into the closet. "I can see you're not like most of the girls who've come through here. Your skin and face have not been hardened by years of street life."

"Thank you," Ava said.

"And I saw you making a list of healthy foods to eat." Ava sat in silence—she hadn't realized anyone was taking such notice of her movements, but was delighted that she made a good impression.

"You'll be fine." Mama Etu smiled with a nod of approval. "We're going to get you deep breathing and stretching in no time. I've been looking for someone to train to help me teach the yoga classes. Are you interested?"

"I'd like that very much, but I've only been to three yoga classes."

"No problem."

"Also, I've enrolled in school, so I'll need scheduling accommodations."

"Okay, it's a plan. Let's get you moving and stretching on a daily basis and then we'll take the next steps."

Ava rolled up her mat, grateful for more opportunities for growth and that the noise of the women talking covered the sounds of her protesting stomach that knew it was lunch time.

CHAPTER 23

The smile spread across her face before she could stop it. Her cell phone buzzing at four pm was always the highlight of her day no matter how rough the day had been. London took a deep breath before pressing the green accept button.

"Hello there Khalil, how are you?"

Khalil's goal was to be patient and pleasant but to remain focused and to the point. The last time he and London were together had indeed confirmed they were no longer in a relationship or friendship. He had no idea why London had left him a message to call her.

"I'm doing well London, I'm returning your call. How can I help you?"

"Wow, must we be so formal?"

He took a deep breath not wanting to let his impatience reign.

"I actually have a lot of work to do and I don't want to be rude London, what is it that you needed?"

"Khalil, I'm not trying to bother or upset you. I wanted to talk with you, so we can clear the air between us, so at le-"

"Pardon my interruption. The air was pretty clear to me when you ended our last meeting with a threat."

"Khalil, I did not threaten you, is that really how you took my words?"

"We're too old to play games London. You know where I come from and the words you used, '*you haven't heard the last from me*', was definitely a threat. So what are you calling for today, London, to make good on your threat?"

"Khalil, I am so, so sorry for saying that. I didn't mean anything by it. I was hurt by the things you said and how abruptly you ended our relationship. I didn't know what else to say."

He could hear the crack in her voice and her attempt to hold back tears. His heart softened in that very moment, but he didn't want to lead her on in anyway.

"Do you hear what you just said. What would have been so hard about using the words you just spoke from your mouth instead of threatening me?"

She sucked back tears and began speaking softly.

"Khalil, you're right. I didn't know how to say those words. I was hurt and angry, so the wrong words took over. I'm just going to get to the point. I miss you and I want to know if there's an opportunity for us to start over?"

He wanted to be careful and emphatic with his words at the same time.

"London, I know the work you've done to reinvent yourself. You're an amazing woman and you have a lot to share, but a relationship between us is not possible." He waited for her to respond, to the point of him having to say, "London, are you there?"

"Yes I'm here. Thank you, Khalil, for being so honest and upfront. Is it a hard blow, yes, is it hard to accept, yes? But at least I don't have to wonder or play any games with myself. One thing I've learned over these years is the power of acceptance. It might take me a minute to get it together, but I can do it."

"Yes you can London. You take care."

"You do the same Khalil, bye."

Khalil ended the call and rested against the back of his chair. "I pray her acceptance comes sooner than later."

CHAPTER 23

Ava had been home and working sixty days at Abigail House and life was good. Her father was making good progress with his rehabilitation—Eli had a few more weekend stays at home before he could come home and be able to function with minimal assistance.

She enjoyed the holidays she had so greatly missed. Mama had outdone herself with Thanksgiving dinner at the house. All of her aunts and cousins were there from both sides of her family. Some of her cousins around her age had lots of questions about her being in jail. She was glad to share the experiences with her with them, warning them to being mindful of every situation that may seem innocent on the surface, but was actually some drama waiting to happen. Khalil had given her a beautiful charm bracelet for Christmas, bringing her to tears explaining why he chose each charm. New Year's Eve was a quaint celebration with her parents, Khalil and a few family members having a game night; including Ava's favorite card game, spades.

Ava and Khalil spent time at the gym, taking walks, and dining while getting to know each other.

She smiled as she thought about how Khalil assigned himself as her personal trainer and the results were paying off. Running a hand over her pancake-flat stomach, she could feel the faint touch of the ripples that were an indication of a developing six-pack. She was in the best shape of her life.

"Ms. Ava, someone's at the front desk for you," Zola announced, peeking her head in Ava's room, and breaking her moment of reflection.

"Okay, thanks. I'll be right down." Ava's heart raced as she thought it was Khalil coming to walk with her to the gym.

The young man at the front desk dressed in tight fighting black pants, sneakers, a bike helmet with a company's insignia, thin jacket and back pack, handed Ava an envelope. Ava signed for a manila envelope with a note folded and taped on top. On the way out the door, after grabbing his bike, the courier turned back to Ava while holding the door open and nodded in the direction of the street, "The gentleman in the car said to read the note on top."

Paul Jakes sneered as Ava's sights set across the street on a white Lexus sedan.

"Congratulations on your new life, Miss Penwood. Enjoy my gift to you." He yelled with a tip of his hat, Jakes drove away.

Ava wondered why Paul Jakes would be dropping anything off to her, especially at her job. She patted her pants pockets, searching for her phone to call Khalil, and remembered she left it upstairs.

"That's a nice car that guy was in," the lady at the desk commented.

"Yeah it was." Ava said, turning slowly to go up the stairs and opening the taped note.

Since we're in the habit of receiving envelopes, here's one to let you know, that your hero hasn't always been trying to save you.

* * *

"Just one more dude, come on, I know there's one more in you." From the moment Ava entered the gym, she heard Khalil and Walé shouting like marine soldiers. "One more," Khalil yelled. "You got this."

Moving like her feet were on fire, Ava reached the pair. She could see every vein in Khalil's body pulsating as he attempted to push up the last press.

Khalil released a groan as he forced the three-hundred-pound barbell above his body. As his spotter, Walé helped him put the equipment in place.

Khalil jumped up from the bench, snatching up his t-shirt and exposing his glistening chest, revealing a pink discoloration on his umber-toned skin with an unusual shape—like a barn house with a steeple.

Sweat from her hastened walk, dripped into Ava's eyes, and her heart sank into the pit of her stomach. She frowned at the sight of the blemish, hot tears brimming her lash line. Her body stiffened as she stood with the envelope in hand courtesy of Paul Jakes, her fiery gaze fixed on Khalil.

Pulling his shirt down, Khalil moved over to Ava. "Hey, you ok, what's wrong?"

Ava dipped away from Khalil's reach. Extracting the contents of the envelope, she threw the handful of images at Khalil's chest, and the pictures floated to the floor.

Walé and Khalil glanced between Ava and the scattered photos.

Stepping closer to him and snatching up his t-shirt. "What's wrong is this, you bastard!" Ava yelled as she punched the blemish on his skin. "I kept wondering …" her voice cracked as she hollered, barely able to speak through the tears. "Why you seemed so familiar. I couldn't put my finger on it until now. It was you! You were the other person in the basement, you were the one who left with Penny to go to the store. I remember you lifting up your shirt and that funny looking mark on your skin."

Walé picked up the photos while Khalil tried to calm Ava down.

"Wait, Ava, baby, listen," Khalil pleaded as he reached for her hand. "Please listen to me."

"It was you. You're how I got to the hospital. You didn't even have enough balls to take me inside the emergency room. You left me. You left me like I was nothing on a bench outside the hospital entrance, hoping someone came out to find me. Look at the pictures, Khalil. Don't lie. And who had to tell me the truth? Paul Jakes, that's who!"

Khalil grabbed her arms, and Ava pulled away from his grasp.

Ava maneuvered through the machines toward the front door as Khalil followed close behind.

Ava turned, narrowing her eyes on Khalil. "Don't you ever in your miserable life call me Baby or Ava." She stormed toward the door, snatching her arm away from him every time he attempted to touch her.

Outside the gym, Khalil pivoted to get in front of her and blocking her into a corner in the gym's lobby area.

"Ava, please let me explain."

"Explain what, Khalil?" She questioned, tears drenching her face as she sobbed. She leveled a steely glare on the man she grew to love.

"Please, you gotta let me explain. I'll tell you everything," Khalil pleaded, his breathing labored from the chase. "Yes, it was me in the basement that night, and I did take you to the emergency room. I didn't know what else to do. I didn't want to get in any trouble, but you were walking around outside, and I knew something was wrong. I was scared, but I couldn't leave you. Taking you to the emer—"

"Get out of my face. All this time you've been wining and dining me, calling me baby, talking about how much you care for me. None of this, none of it, was about me. This wall all about clearing your motherf—"

"Stop it! I'm so sorry." His eyes became glassy with tears as he begged her to listen. "I swear it wasn't like that. Please, let's go sit down. I need you to hear me out."

In one swift motion, Ava pushed Khalil out of her space and charged in the direction of Abigail House.

"Ava, please," Khalil yelled across the distance, holding his forehead in both hands. She turned to face him. She pointed her finger, took a deep breath, and spoke slowly.

"Don't ever call me, speak to me, or come to my house. As a matter of fact, don't speak my name again as long as you live. All this time you were playing a dangerous game, Khalil.   Your charade is over. If you ever talk to me again, I'm gonna tell the whole world who you really are and ruin your life. I promise you." She turned and ran towards the entrance of the building.

I'm so stupid. Ava scolded herself for not remembering sooner. Everything she thought she knew about Khalil and her dreams of their lives together came crashing down with one visit from the enemy.

CHAPTER 25

Khalil knew it was too late to show up at Bernie's house, but it didn't matter, he had to say what was on his chest. He rang the doorbell and paced the front porch.

"Who's at my door at this hour?" Bernie yelled from the other side of the oak door. "It's eleven o'clock." The door swung open and sleepy eyes and a grimace met Khalil—not Bernie's usual look. Glancing at the watch that didn't match his flannel pajamas, Bernie leveled a steely glare on his protégé.

"Is there an emergency?" Bernie's snapped, his uninviting tone causing the tears to flow that Khalil held back.

"Bernie, I lied," Khalil mumbled. "I *knew* who she was."

Bernie stood in the doorway; his apparent sleepiness was traded for a look of confusion. "What do you mean you knew her?"

"I was in the basement that night. I took her to the hospital."

"The Penwood woman?"

Khalil nodded, his heart pounded as he recounted the story. "I dropped her off at the emergency room door. She didn't remember who I was. I knew she wasn't at fault, but I couldn't tell you how I knew.

I tried my best to get her out of jail because of what happened. I'm so sorry."

Bernie's shoulders dropped as he shook his head. "Come on son, let's sit down."   Reaching for Khalil's arm, he ushered him into the house, kicking the door closed with a foot.

Khalil handed Bernie the envelope with the pictures and followed him to the living room , dropping down into the leather sofa.

Bernie thumbed the envelope open, peered at Khalil, then went to the kitchen. Upon his return, he handed Khalil a cup of water, which he poured down his throat like he had been in the desert for weeks dying of thirst.

Setting the glass down, he examined Bernie's face, having little hope for any empathy. "Bernie, I need to tell you everything."

"I'm listening." Bernie sat the envelope down on the table. He picked up a teacup, crossed his legs, and reclined in the oversized soft forest green chair.

"I was in my second year at Johan Marshall and I was down state that weekend doing some research for a case study. I met the guy Monty in the convenience store that was near the building I was visiting. There was nothing menacing about him at all. Nothing about him said he had the intentions of what happened. So when he invited me to his house for a kickback that night, I didn't think anything of it. It seemed like a great time to unwind before I went back to the city the next day. When I got there, I could almost feel something was off. The only people there was the guy Nook, who died in the police chase, Ava, Terri and the girl Penny. I wasted cranberry juice on my shirt and that's how Ava saw and remembered my burn. The girl Penny said she was going to the store to get some drinks and I could go with her because they sold t-shirts."

Bernie took a sip from the cup, and Khalil used the back of a hand to wipe the moisture that collected underneath his nose. "She came to the gym today with the pictures and mentioned my scar. She didn't remember me, but she remembered *that*."

"What do you mean about your skin, son?"

"It's a scar from a motorcycle accident," Khalil explained as he rubbed the spot through his shirt. "I got burned and the color never came back. It's the most sensitive part on my body. It reminds me to push and be strong." He rubbed his torso through his shirt. "I don't know where Jakes got the pictures, but he made damn sure that Ava received them." Khalil lowered his gaze, and Bernie took another sip of his beverage. "This could ruin me."

"So, now you're concerned about being ruined?" Bernie asked, with a chuckle.

Khalil's heart sank even further as heat from embarrassment crept up his neck. "I don't even care about any of that. I love Ava. I want to be with her for the rest of my life and now she won't even speak to me."

"I can't say I blame her. Do you think she realizes what other implications this could initiate because of *your* selfishness?"

Wiping a hand over head, Khalil held the back of his neck and lifted his gaze from the floor. "It took me all day to come talk to you, Bernie. You're more than a mentor to me. You're like my father."

Bernie sucked in a deep breath and blew it out. Shaking his head, he threw up a hand. "Keep talking, Khalil."

The sound of resignation made Khalil shudder—he never wanted to disappoint Bernie after all that he had done to help him get to where he was, yet at the same time all that mattered was how he could get Ava to come back to him. "The guy Nook went outside to smoke a cigarette and me and Penny left to go to the store. I didn't know what Monty had planned. By the time we got back from the store, an ambulance and police cars were everywhere. I saw Ava walking around in a daze. Penny said we should leave and let the police figure out she was missing."

"So, how did you end up getting her in the car and taking her to the emergency room?" Bernie inquired. "This girl, Penny, just left you hanging with the bag?"

"That's what happened. I couldn't just leave her, but we got to the hospital, I got scared. I sat Ava on a bench outside the sliding doors where someone would see, and I just left her there."

Bernie placed the teacup on the end table beside the chair. "Do you hear yourself?"

"I knew it had to be an act of fate when we got the anonymous tip," Khalil insisted, ignoring Bernie's question. "I always wanted to come forth and say something. I finally told my mother about the incident, she told me to finish school and forget about it. But, how could I forget? I never forgot about what happened."

The room was quiet as the two sat across from each other. Khalil replayed the whole scene and all of what he said in his mind.

"Take off your jacket, tie and shoes and stretch out on this couch." Bernie stood from his seat, ambled to a nearby closet, and came back with a blanket.

"Am I supposed to sleep?" Khalil leveled a puzzled gaze on Bernie as he sat on the edge of the couch.

Bernie left the room again and returned with two small pills and a cup of water. "Take these. You're gonna have the headache from hell in the morning if you don't get under this blanket and get some rest. I'm sure you can't tell, but I'm pissed. I appreciate you telling me everything, but this is a mess.

"Bernie, man lis—," Khalil protested.

"Take the pills and lay down," Bernie demanded. "We'll see how to clean this up over breakfast in the morning."

Khalil conceded, took off his shoes, and laid down.

Bernie covered him with the blanket, rubbed his shoulder, like a father comforting a young boy, and turned off the light. "We'll figure this out. I'll see you in the morning. Good night."

"Good night." Khalil murmured, exhausted.

Khalil laid on the couch, listening to the echoes of Ava's voice, imagining her running away from him, and wondering if there was any way he could get her back. He proved to be a man of his word before when he won the retrial, but would it be enough to redeem himself back into Ava's good graces?

CHAPTER 26

The weekend seemed like a distant future as Ava's heart ached as she spent the rest of the week mostly alone, outside of the yoga classes she taught, until her mother picked her up for family time. She avoided all staff and residents so she wouldn't have to answer any questions or lie. There was no way she could tell anyone who Khalil was now and she was certain her parents didn't need to know what she discovered.

She was grateful for the back-to-back classes she had to teach that kept her busy. She had begun to build a great friendship with Zola. It was nice having a friend again. She had reached out to a couple of her friends from high school for reconnection but her efforts were futile. She had decided to make new friends going forward. In her one-on-one times with Zola she learned the twenty-year-old had served time for killing her mother's boyfriend after years of him raping her. Helping her through her anger issues through yoga, journaling and meditation was a great distraction for Ava.

Sylvia stopped Ava as she reached the exit to the house. "Are you okay, Ava?" Sylvia asked, concerned etched into her face.

"Not really, but I don't feel like talking about it." Ava pushed the door open to leave.

"Alright, Ms. Ava," Sylvia said, clasping her hands together. "I hope you start feeling better over the weekend. I'll see you on Monday"

"I promise I'll be working on it, Ms. Sylvia." Ava waved goodbye, speeding toward the awaiting vehicle.

The car door opened, and the smell of fried chicken and mild sauce hit her in the face. She remained quiet, taking in deep breaths to stay calm as Eli and Vera laughed and retold the stories about the day's events.

Ava faked a smile and pretended to be happy. With no energy or interest to talk, the ride home was too tough to participate in conversation.

Ava watched the buildings whiz by as they zigzagged down Pulaski and then Cicero. In her periphery she noticed her father's attention on her as he glanced back from the front passenger seat. She dreaded knowing that there would be a conversation before the night ended. She had no desire to talk about Khalil. She wanted to forget about any notion that he helped her gain her freedom—he abandoned her and not knowing what happened after he left. Glancing at her father's profile she knew he'd want to talk, and she wasn't ready for anything more than the tears to stop falling.

* * *

Ava laid across her bed, after telling her parents she wasn't feeling well and didn't want to eat. A gentle tap on the door broke the silence and her racing thoughts.

"Yeah," Ava mumbled, turning toward the sound.

"It's ya' daddy," Eli declared. "I need to see why my baby girl isn't hungry. What's the matter?"

Ava sat up and wiped the tears from her face. "Come in."

Eli entered the room, and Ava leaned back onto the headboard willing the tears to stay. Claiming a seat in a chair near the end of the bed, Eli tapped a spot on the comforter and encouraged her to move closer.

Still wiping her face, she scooted over, and offered her father a weak smile.

"I knew something was wrong with my baby girl on the ride home," Eli confessed as he patted Ava's knee. "You ready to talk about it?"

"I—I don't know," Ava stammered, her voice shaking. "You know I've never kept anything from you since I was little."

"Let's not start now. Whatever it is, no matter how good, bad, or ugly, ya' daddy is right here like he's always been."

Ava's lip quivered as she started bawling, unable to control the flow of tears that fell.

Eli handed her tissue from the box on the nightstand and took another and helped her blot the moisture that streamed down her cheeks.

"I feel tricked, used, and deceived," Ava cried as she clasped her hands in a position of prayer in front of her mouth. "I mean I feel stupid and I'm mad as hell." Ava's voice grew louder until she was near shouting.

Eli was a calm-spirited man, who learned early in life to let silence have its place. He continued to tap the cane using his fingertips as if he were playing an instrument.

"When everything happened that night in Monty's basement, there were more people there than me, Terri and Monty," Ava explained through sniffles. "When we first got there, it was Monty, his two friends, me, Terri, and the girl Penny who set everything up."

Eli nodded, continuing to fidget. "One of the guys went outside to smoke a cigarette. The other guy and the girl Penny went to the store. Everything happened while they were gone, so I didn't see them again. The guy that was outside smoking, died in the car accident when the police chased Monty in his grandmother's car."

Eli steadied his gaze on Ava, then nodded as if he were letting her know he was waiting for more.

"Daddy, the guy who left with Penny was Khalil. I can't believe that it was Khalil."

Eli sat back, shaking his head, then leveled a concerned look on his daughter.

"Your friend-boy? The lawyer? The one who got you out of jail?"

Eli stood and ambled to the door. "Vera! Vera-Ann, come in here please," Eli bellowed.

Vera came to the door drying her hands with a kitchen towel. "What's going on in here? What's wrong, Ava baby?"

Tears sprung from Ava's eyes like a waterfall.

Eli reclaimed his spot in the chair next to Ava, looking at Vera and continuing to shake his head.

"Is someone gonna tell me what's going on?"

Ava choked on her words. Eli took a deep breath. "Baby, the lawyer gentlemen that has taken a liking to our daughter, was one of the perpetrators in the basement the night everything happened."

Vera dropped the towel and covered her mouth with both hands.

Ava bent over and rested her head in her hands.

"What are you saying? How the hell did he become the lawyer to get you out of jail? How did you find out?"

Ava lifted her eyes to meet her mother's. "Paul Jakes dropped off the photos as proof. I don't know, Mama. I'm mad and I'm hurt, but I love him. I'm in love with a man who acted like he was trying to help me. He dropped me off at that emergency room and left me, like I was nothing and went on and never told me anything. He's been pretending this whole time. Why is this happening? It wasn't enough that I almost got raped, then went to jail, only to get set free by one of the men that started this whole terrible part of my life?"

Vera sat down and wrapped Ava in her arms as she trembled. "We're going to get to the bottom of this. Okay, baby? We're going to work through it. We're gonna get through like we do everything else."

Eli stood with his cane, smoothed a hand over Ava's hair, kissed the crown of her head, and left the room.

Vera comforted Ava as she hugged and rocked her until she was ready to speak.

"Mama, what do I do?" Ava asked, lifting her head off of her mother's shoulder. "I love this man. He's been taking such good care of me and has taught me so many things. He's patient and I feel like he cares for me. I just don't understand how I didn't remember him from before. Now, it seems as if it was all a lie. Could he really have been pretending this whole time?" Ava rested her head back on Vera's shoulder and wept.

"You know baby, life has a funny way of working things out," Vera said as she caressed Ava's back. "This big old Universe always has something moving and stirring. We'll get to the bottom of this."

"Okay, Mama." Ava wiped her face and gave her mother a kiss on the cheek. "Thank you for listening. I'm gonna lay down now."

"Alright, baby." Vera eased off the bed, picked up the towel, and turned to her daughter. "Ava, so you're saying when everything happened Khalil wasn't in the basement?"

Ava rested against a pillow and nodded the answer to her mother's question.

"He was gone with Penny. I guess by the time they got back from the store everything had happened. I only remembered who he was because of something he did at the gym. I went to show him the pictures. He has a scar on his body that looks like a house. When I saw the scar, it hit me that he was one of the boys from that night."

"Well, get some rest. Your dad is home this weekend and we'll get this straightened out."

A shiver snaked up Ava's spine—she didn't know what to expect from her father. She remembered the dark look in his eyes when he was angry, and a situation needed to be settled.

Eli knew how to solve a problem and never be in the vicinity to see its end. He was never one to let anything slide that hurt his community. Ava was non-negotiable community, she was his baby girl. He would see the gates of hell before he let anyone hurt her.

Ava heard Vera's footsteps stop in the hallway. She eased to the doorway to see if her mother was okay, but what she heard next confirmed her worst fear.

"Okay, Brother Malik." Eli's tone was gruff and unpleasant. "Yeah, bring Fred and Hambone with you. I'll let you know when. Thank you. I appreciate you."

Malik, Fred and Hambone were former Black Panther members and daddy's friends. They were more like uncles. She had just seen them at the Thanksgiving celebration which was more of a welcome home party for Ava.   Calling them after what she had just told her father couldn't be good.

Ava heard her mother murmuring something. Maybe she was saying a prayer like Ava was. She had only heard her father yell three times in her entire life. Sleep wouldn't come easy. Now, she had to decide if she wanted to forgive Khalil or let the consequences her father had in store to teach him the lesson he should have learned years ago

CHAPTER 27

"Are you serious?" Khalil shouted as he spoke to Bernie. "No disrespect, Bernie, but I've never lied to you before."

"You're right, Benson, so why start now? And with a case so delicate? This is what I call really bad timing."

"How many times have I lied *for* you to cut a corner to get the win?" A wrinkle creased the center of Bernie's forehead—Khalil knew from past experiences, that look meant he'd struck a nerve. Khalil stood, staring at the papers Bernie had prepared. "You wait until I walk in here Monday morning to tell me I'm suspended? Without pay? I came to you on Thursday night."

"Khalil, do you know what your selfishness could cost us?" Bernie yelled, leaning into Khalil's face. "*This* could ruin us. Not just you, but the HUB, all of us. The fact that Paul Jakes found this information could cause more damage than good. You know damn well this isn't the end of this."

"Okay, so instead of us coming up with a strategy to prepare for the fight, you take me completely out of the battle? This is unreal."

"Your hands aren't clean," Bernie explained, leveling an angry glare on Khalil. "You're standing here like we don't have a tornado coming against us. Do you really believe your arch enemy is going to keep some damaging information like this under wraps?" Bernie said, waving his arms above his head. "Hell, it's too big for him to even blackmail us. You're out here playing knight in shining armor, but you're the bull in a China shop."

Khalil's nostrils flared as he filled his chest with air. Tension built in his back and shoulders as he sat on the edge of his seat in the oversized chair in front of Bernie. "What do you think I'm supposed to do with this? My father taught me loyalty is rewarded, not to be pissed on. You both taught me to be a man and stand up for myself. All that he didn't get to teach me, you taught me the rest. I've been loyal without question and honestly speaking, I feel like you're dumping on that now."

"So, you don't think any kind of reprimand is in order? None? There are four photographs that show you getting Miss Penwood, our client, out of your car, sitting her on the bench in front of a hospital entrance and driving off. The conflict of interest is beyond question. With the history you and Jakes have, do you think he's going to sit with this?"

Khalil leaned forward and put his head in his hands. Wiping his palms down across his face, he cupped his mouth. After drawing in a deep breath, he stood. "Bernie, I love you like a father, but here is where I draw the line. I don't think this suspension is right."

Bernie nodded. "I understand. It is what it is and it's gonna be what it's gonna be." He eased against the back of the chair.

Khalil turned on his heels and stormed out of the office. After the victory of winning Ava's case, the HUB decided to press full speed ahead with researching other cases that had been tampered with by the medical examiner, Dr. Jed Mills. Khalil was supposed to be the lead on most of those cases. The time was ripe, and the can was open, so there was no need to quit or wait. This would be a landmark class action suit against the County hospital, and Khalil was primed for the fight. He knew every staff member at the HUB would be preparing for the match of their careers.

How are they taking on Goliath without me?

* * *

Days had passed since Khalil had stepped foot into the office at the HUB, too many if anyone were to ask him—he wasn't used to not being a part of the preparation process on any cases. Wednesday morning came, and a renewed sense of responsibility with it.

"Good morning, Ms. Helen," Khalil greeted as he breezed by. "You're looking lovely as usual."

"Thank you, Khalil."

Khalil inhaled a deep breath as he made his stop at Bernie's office doorway. Taking up the full space of the entrance, Khalil cleared his throat to announce his presence.

"Hey, Bernie. Can I come in?"

"Of course, son. I'm surprised and glad to see you. I didn't know what to expect after our last conversation. Have a seat." Khalil took a seat in one of the leather winged-backed chairs facing Bernie's desk.

"Yeah, about that," Khalil said with a chuckle.

"And to be upfront, the suspension had to take its course with the groundwork for anything that may come our way. In the event those pictures got into the wrong hands or made it to the media, we don't need any appearance of impropriety."

Khalil nodded in agreement. Bernie folded his hands on top of the desk, an indication to Khalil that he could take a turn to speak.

"Alright, Bernie, here it is. I accept the suspension for what it is, and we don't have to discuss it again." He took a deep breath and sat tall, slapping his hands into a resting position on his thighs. "I came here today to tell you that I'm leaving the HUB."

Bernie swallowed hard and adjusted his tie as he maintained eye contact with Khalil. "But before I go, I'd like to partner with you and finish the class action suit against the County ... under my own firm-KB Benson and Associates."

Bernie leaned forward, moving the teacup to one side of the desk. "And associates, huh?" He nodded, laced his fingers, and clasped his hands again.

"Yes, I'm leaving, and Martin is coming with me."

Bernie leaned back again, rubbing his forehead. "Benson, what's this. What's really going on?" He slid a hand over his face and tapped his chin with a clenched fist.

"Is there a problem?" Khalil inquired, surprised that Bernie wasn't more supportive of the idea.

"What the hell did you think I was going to say to a ballsy ass statement like that."

"Look Bernie, I watched you for years before you recruited me. You've trained me to never settle and always take it up top. This is a win-win for both of us. It sets me up in my new firm and puts you higher on the legal ladder in the city, hell, higher up on the state ladder for that matter. This will be the first time a Non-Profit took it to the hilt. You know we can win this thing and you know we can both come out on top."

The salt and peppered haired man sighed and took a few moments to respond. His silence didn't sway Khalil—Bernie taught all of his staff to bask in the spaces where there weren't any words spoken.

"It's the signal that lets you know you got 'em, and they don't have any room to move." Bernie would say.

That moment seemed like an eternity before Bernie spoke. "Okay, we know the non-profit rules, we can't charge the full 33%, but we'll create our usual billing for service, hours and court fees. We've already found nine cases, so that means the pot is growing. What are you talking about on the split for KB Benson and Associates?"

"Look Bernie, I'm not trying to hurt you here, you've done a lot for me, and I've been loyal to you. Let's go 60 for you 40 for me. That'll be what I need to cover my overhead and pay Martin and Roman." Khalil was leaning forward with clasped hands, his elbows rested on his knees.

"Oh yeah, Roman, what's the plan with his services? He's your childhood friend so I assume he's going to start helping you with cases."

"You're right about that, but I'd never cut him out of his money. He can work for the both of us. Does that work for you?" Khalil waited for Bernie's response.

"That works Benson, that works just fine." "We're definitely going to need him. The whole team will need to be on deck to win this battle."

Khalil stood and extended a hand to Bernie. "We got this. We need to move quickly. I don't know if Jakes has any more photos or if he copied them. We have to shine the light on him before he shines it on me."

Bernie stood he reached for a stack of files in the corner of his desk, placing them down in front of the bold, young attorney. "We may not have to worry too much about Jakes. It seems he's been a busy little spider, weaving a web of his own. In the nine cases we have so far, Mills and Jakes show up in five. It seems they've been working together for at least six years, as far as we can see."

"Jack pot." Khalil lightly pounded the stack of files and picked them up. "Can Karyn make a copy of all these for me?"

Bernie leveled a hard gaze on Khalil, crossing his arms over his chest. "I'll be damned. I knew at some point you were going off on your own. I was hoping it would've been after I retired, and you wouldn't become my competition."

They both chuckled as he walked around his desk, reaching to pat Khalil on the back. Khalil met his mentor with a hug.

"I won't come for you too hard, old man. Thanks for everything you've taught me, and I know there's always more to learn."

Bernie tapped his own temple with his index finger. "Ah, the student has become the teacher." Laughter continued between the two as Bernie patted Khalil on his shoulder.

The few days at home gave Khalil the opportunity to come up with this plan. Now, he had to figure out how to get Ava back into his life.

CHAPTER 28

"What the hell are you doing, Benson?" Paul Jakes spun around and dropped his briefcase as he came face to face with Khalil. "What are you doing here, sneaking up on me? This garage is private company property, how the hell did you get in here?"

Khalil towered at least a head over Jakes as he stepped into his personal space. "Don't worry about any of that you slimy, no backbone having piece of shit." Khalil's voice was deep and slow. His eyes narrowed and steady, his stance unmovable. "I know it was you who gave those pictures to Ava, and you're going to tell me who gave them to you."

Jakes straightened his blazer and adjusted his stature as if he was attempting to grow to his opponent's height, however his effort made Khalil laugh to himself.

"You have your sources, and I have my own," Jakes sneered. "You're going down in flames, Benson. You had no business trying that case with the conflict of interest involved. I found the pictures to prove it."

In one swift motion, Khalil reached out with both hands and grabbed Jakes's collar, pulling him up on his loafer covered tiptoes. "Hear me now and hear me good. You're going to tell me where you got those pictures from and you're going to tell me now." Jakes gripped Khalil's hands, trying to loosen his hold on him. "You're going to tell me and we're not going to ask again." Roman stepped from the shadows, tapping a silver 9mm in its holster.

Jakes body began to tremble under Khalil's grasp. "Who gave you these pictures and where are the copies?" His words were calculated. His face was so close to Jakes, he could see the retina lining in his pupil. "Don't make this become a crime scene."

Khalil pulled his collar even tighter, despite the complexion of the usually pale Jakes he was turning beet red.

"Okay, Okay," he said as he choked. "In my briefcase everything's in my briefcase."

Roman stepped around the two men and bent to open the black, leather briefcase. He grabbed the USB and two envelopes.

"I got everything, B. Let's ride." Roman folded the envelopes, tucking them in the back of his belt as he stood.

"I'm going to tell you this for the last fucking time. If you every mumble so much as a syllable to Ava, it will be the last words you ever speak. I've been doing some research. Do you know I found out that you and Dr. Mills had a thing going on to protect the hospital from medical malpractice cases? Would you like to know how many cases *I* found?" Khalil glared at Jakes as a wicked grin spread across Khalil's face. "I'm going to get you, your father, Dr. Mills, and every rotten doctor at that hospital that caused someone's death. *You won't beat me.*" Khalil pushed him with a thud against the car when he released him.

"You're finished, Benson." Jakes yelled as he rubbed the red ring around his neck. "I'm going to get you and the HUB once and for all. You think you know something, but you don't know a damn thing. You're not getting away with this. We're all coming for you, so you betta grow eyes in the back of your smug ass head. You're not getting away with this, you bastard."

Khalil slowly turned towards Jakes before stepping into the open elevator with Roman waiting. "I just did. Now, let's see who comes out on top. You and that medical examiner are going down." Jakes sat on the ground leaning against his car, and the elevator closed with Khalil and Roman never taking their eyes off Jakes.

* * *

Two week later . . .

"Paul Jakes II, the son of Paul Jakes Sr., of the PP & Jakes top law firm in Chicago, was found unresponsive in his Oak Lawn condominium this morning by his housekeeper. He was transported to Christ Hospital and remains in a coma. We have no further information to report. The family respectfully requests no calls or visits at this time so they can deal with this matter privately. We'll update you as we receive information. This is KBET channel 6 reporting in Chicago."

Roman laid the file down he held in his hand. Khalil sat back in the Ivory leather chair and began rocking.

"Can you believe this?" Roman leveled a hard gaze at Khalil as he spoke, his sandy locs hanging loose around his shoulders. "You know this is some bullshit, right? Found unresponsive my ass. He was really supposed to be found dead."

"Found unresponsive, what the hell could've happened to him?" Khalil exclaimed. "In a coma? Damn!"

"Either someone was trying to shut him up, or he was making an attempt to not tell something he wasn't supposed to tell." Martin chimed from his standing position next to the table they were gathered at.

"Think about it man, we now have sixteen cases that prove Dr. Mills tampered with the files. We can also prove Jakes involvement in twelve of those cases." Martin tapped on the files spread out across the table as he spoke.

"Can you believe this man? You start your own law firm and out the gate you file a class action case against the city, with evidence to prove it. Man listen."

"You're right about it my friend, but in light of the news we just heard we have to capitalize on this." Khalil stopped rocking and sat up tall, beating a fist into an open palm. "How many more subpoenas need to go out?

"All the families, but four have been served, due to a change of address. I'll have the new addresses by the end of the day tomorrow." Martin was still standing, looking at a list he picked up.

"What about medical personnel? Have we located Mills yet?"

"We still don't know where this dude is. You know I'm still looking for him." Roman tapped the table lightly with a slightly clenched fist.

"I know if anybody can find him, you can. Let's take a look at what we have. Of the sixteen cases, we have someone to come forth and represent the deceased of twelve families. We can prove Dr. Mills changed the cause of death dating back nineteen years to clear the hospital of any damages." Khalil tapped a pen against a legal pad full of written information.

"In eight cases, the families thought there was something shady that happened in their family member's death, and Jakes took on all the cases, winning them for the hospital." Martin echoed while searching a file, his finger going up and down the summary page on top."

"Rome, I wonder how much money Jakes has in his bank account?" Khalil took a swallow from his water bottle. "I'm already ahead of you." He slid Khalil a single sheet of paper across the table from the file that was in his hand.

Khalil snatched up the sheet and held it right in front of his face. "One million plus in his bank account. What the fu-?"

"And that's not all." Roman slid another piece of paper across the table out of the same file. "I found this. It's an annuity."

Khalil stood and reached for the document. "Two million dollars, you have got to be kidding me."

"You ready for the kicker?" Martin asked.

"Of the twelve cases we have, Jakes was the lead prosecutor and won against the hospital, but on the other four, they were settled out of court and out of the newspaper by, guess who?" He asked sarcastically

"Let me take a wild guess here." Khalil placed his fingertips against his temples. "These cases were settled by Papa Paul Jakes and his firm."

"Bingo, you are the winner." His partner pointed to him with a smile. "Those cases netted PP & Jakes, a cool three million plus."

The childhood friends, and new business partner all spoke in unison, "found unresponsive?"

Khalil chuckled, "Martin, man, it's great having you back. I hope everything turns out well with your dad.

Martin walked over to where Khalil was sitting, putting a hand on his shoulder and looking him square in the face.

"Thanks man. I appreciate you being patient with me and letting me work through it. I don't know if it's all over, but the dust has settled for now. Let's get this work."

Khalil settled back in the chair, tapping his fingertips against his thighs, staring at the wall and nodding.

"What's up, B?" Roman asked.

"Man, I'm just thinking of the irony of this entire situation. A man in a coma is how all this started."

Roman was now leaning back in the leather office chair slightly moving side to side, with his head turned to the ceiling. "What I'm more worried about is where did Jakes get those pictures of you and Ava from. We don't know if there are more copies out there, or how it may come back to haunt us." He slowly turned and put his elbows on the table, looking between both men. "Somebody in that hospital gave that footage to Jakes. We have to find out who and soon." Both Khalil and Martin nodded in agreement.

Paul Jakes was transferred to an assisted nursing facility in a vegetative state unable to speak or communicate in any way what happened to him. Khalil, Martin and the Hub moved urgently gathering information to prove the hospital's negligence in the one the largest settlements against a hospital in the state of Illinois' history. Everything was moving in the right direction in Khalil's world except the treasure he desired most; Ava

CHAPTER 29

Ava was glad Vera offered to pick her up from Abigail House on her way home. Their home smelled of deep southern cooking. Vera made the celebration special for her husband's homecoming. She baked a homemade chocolate cake, ordered chicken, fish and beef ribs—all of Eli's favorites. She picked him up from the center early, reminding him he wouldn't have a meal like this for a while since he was still recovering. By the time they got to Ava, the festivities had already begun as they sang their own loud Westside rendition of Al Green's Love and Happiness.

Ava enjoyed seeing her parents so happy. She reflected on how much her mother had been through between her daughter going to prison and her husband having a stroke. Her mother still wore a smile after having weathered all the storms that had come her way by herself. Three years later, their home was beautiful, and she made sure to always practice self-care to maintain her sanity.

Ava missed Khalil. She appreciated having her parents together, being a whole unit again, and thought how perfect it would be if he were there celebrating with them

Eli took a break from two-stepping with his wife and peered over at Ava while he caught his breath, the therapy he had over the last few months in the rehab got him back to the point of dancing again almost better than before. Motioning to Ava to come and sit at the table, she could see concern still etched on his face.

"How are you feeling, baby?" Eli asked quietly, tapping the back of the chair Ava sat in.

"I'm okay, Daddy," Ava replied. "I guess, work is okay, and the classes aren't too challenging yet." Ava pulled her legs and feet into the lotus position in the chair.

"You're just *okay*?" Eli repeated. "What would make it better?"

"What do you mean?"

"Well, if something is just okay, then it can be made better."

Ava's gaze bounced around the room before meeting her father's eyes. "I don't know."

"Would you feel better if Khalil was still around?" Eli asked as if he were reading Ava's mind.

"I miss him so much," Ava confessed. "I'm just scared that I won't be able to believe what he says about anything, especially about that night." Ava ran her index fingers over her thumbs, attempting to diffuse the anxiety that crept in.

"Have you given him a chance to explain?"

"No, sir"

"Even a quick moment to hear his side?" Ava lowered her eyes to the floor waiting for her father to reprimand her for being so stubborn. He had taught her that being hard-headed should have a purpose. At this point, she wasn't so sure that not forgiving Khalil made any sense. "Ava, this is my advice to you—hear him out. You have your own mind that you have to protect. Forgiveness is a tool we have as a way to guard our peace. I've always taught you that." Eli took the cane and moved it outside his legs, letting his hands rest on his thighs. "Vera-Ann" he called out over a shoulder. "Take a break and come in here for a minute."

Vera sat on the footrest next to Eli. He and Vera looked at each other and Eli nodded.

"Ava, me and your dad needed to seek some forgiveness of our own many, many years ago."

Ava settled her feet to the floor, as she waited for the rest of her mother's statement.

"What I'm about to tell you I've never shared before," Vera spoke, her voice just above a whisper.

Ava's glance raced back and forth between her parents. "Wh-What's wrong? Is it serious?"

Vera cleared her throat and released a sigh. "I'm not your daddy's first wife."

"What?" Ava's eyes popped wide, and her mouth dropped. "What do you mean you're not daddy's first wife?"

Vera rubbed her hands along her thighs as if she were wiping them dry. "Without all of the details, your daddy and I met at a Black Panther rally. We were attracted to each other, but nothing happened because he was married." She turned to Eli.

"I was married, but I wasn't happy. My first wife, Cecelia, and I were going through some real rough times and eventually, we separated, and I moved out of the house we lived in. Your mother and I had a few lunches and some phone conversations, but still had to be careful how we moved, because Cecelia and I weren't divorced yet. When I met your mother, she made me laugh and always made me feel like a man. Long story short, Cecelia and I decided to get a divorce. I wanted to start dating your mother, but we thought it would be better to hold off until the divorce was final."

Ava covered her mouth and was slowly shaking her head.

"We thought it was the right thing to do, you know, waiting for the divorce to be final," Vera continued. "As soon as your daddy and I got together I got pregnant with you. Cecelia was pissed at Eli for dating someone so quickly after they broke up. She was a woman scorned and made the weekly meetings hell for us, stirring up gossip and making it seem as if your dad cheated on her. Every week one of the leaders wanted to have a meeting with one of us. It got so crazy, we made the decision to leave the party so we could live in peace and not have me all stressed out while I was pregnant."

Ava glanced back and forth between her parents, her mouth hanging open in disbelief.

"We weren't trying to hurt Cecelia at all. I was out of the house and the divorce proceedings had started. She made it clear to me in no way did she desire to be my wife anymore." Eli adjusted his posture in the wide back chair, sitting up straighter. "I asked her one more time if she wanted to try and work it out, even though I was sweet on your mother. I really wanted to do the right thing, even if it meant me continuing to be unhappy." Eli extended a hand toward Vera, and she smiled as she placed her hand in his

"You see baby, sometimes things in life just happen, you don't plan or prepare for it," Vera explained. "What counts is how you respond to it."

Ava's heart ached— she didn't want to believe that her parents ever withheld anything from her. "That's why y'all left the party?" She pointed to each of her parents and they both nodded their shared response.

"Why are you guys telling me this now? Y'all really could've gone to your graves with *this* secret." Ava sat back in the chair, pouting as though she were a toddler preparing for her next tantrum.

"We're telling you this, baby, because we had to go back to Cecelia and ask for forgiveness. See, when you forgive someone or forgiveness is extended to you, a release happens and where the space was cleared of hate, hurt, or pain, the space is able to be filled with blessings and breakthroughs." Eli leaned forward and reached to grab Ava's hand.

"You betta say it, hon." Vera whispered, with closed eyes, a raised right palm, and nodding as if she were encouraging the preached message.

"I just can't take any more," Ava expressed with a lowered head. "Everybody's got bones in the closet. First Khalil, now you two. I don't even know how I'm supposed to feel right now. All of this is too much. I'm going to bed so I can get my mind together. I love y'all. Good night."

Ava stomped to her room, not looking back even once at her parents. She heard her mother questioning her father just as she stepped into her room. She stood by the open door to eavesdrop on her father's response.

"Do you think we did the right thing by telling her honey?" Vera asked.

"Vera-Ann, we've been freed and cleared of what happened. We've been forgiven and blessed ever since. Ain't no reason to let her live the rest of her life without even trying to have happiness with the young man, but without her forgiving him, she can't go forward. Forgiveness is a part of life and once we understand the power and beauty of it, we'll all be a little better off." "She'll be okay. We did what we were supposed to do."

"Whew." Vera let out with a loud sigh. "Okay, baby, I've always trusted you to lead us on the right path and I won't stop now. You want some of this chocolate cake I made for you, Shugga?"

"Whew is right and you know I do want a piece."

"My baby girl is gonna to be just fine."

Ava could hear the relief in her parent's voice now that they had released their own secret to her. She closed the door, thinking maybe she was hasty in her decision to cut Khalil off. Her parents found happiness—the kind of love she wanted for herself.

If I forgive Khalil, how will I ever trust him again?

CHAPTER 30

Tuesday morning Ava woke up ready to begin her day with a renewed freshness—crying, being sad, missing Khalil, were done as far as she was concerned. The past few weeks had been more than eventful to say the least.

Opening her room door, she found Sylvia with a raised fist as if she were about to knock. Ava couldn't read the expression on her face.

"May I come in?" Sylvia asked. Ava stepped back into the room and sat on the bed.

Sylvia stepped in the room, closed the door, she was holding an envelope.

Ava's heart dropped as she observed her supervisor's eyes turn glassy.

"The guards cleaned out the cell of the old lady that used to be your cellmate. After she passed away, they found this letter in one of the boxes."

Ava's hand shook as she reached for the envelope. Even after Sylvia released it to her, she couldn't make the shaking stop. Peering up at her supervisor, she opened her mouth to say thank you, but nothing came out—the fist-sized lump forming in her throat wouldn't allow her to speak.

One blink and relentless tears began run down her cheeks.

Sylvia sat on the edge of the bed next to her. "Ava, can I say something? If you don't want to talk now it's okay."

Ava nodded in response to Sylvia's question.

Sylvia spoke softly as she placed a hand on Ava's leg. "I can imagine it's hard receiving the news of Ms. Dot's passing. I remember when you first came to see me, you told me how she protected you and how much that meant to you." Ava nodded, and the corners of her lips turned up. "I also remember you telling me how you took care of her when she was diagnosed with cancer."

Ava nodded again and closed her eyes.

"Ms. Dot was very lucky to have you. It seems that it was definitely by God's design, that you were put in the cell with her. Take comfort in knowing for three years, you were both exactly what each other needed." Sylvia stood, bent over and gave her a hug and left the room closing the door behind her.

The sob that was stuck in Ava's throat broke free. Still holding the envelope in her hand, she gently crumpled it as she remembered laughing with Ms. Dot and all the times they looked out for each other making sure they were okay. From her very first day in the cell to the time Ms. Dot saved her in the showers. Even through the tears, she laughed, hearing Dot's voice.

* * *

"Ava put on your clothes and let's go." Ava didn't see the shank in the old woman's hands until she bent down to pick up her flip flops.

"This is my cellie," Ms. Dot informed two women in the showers, one was taller and bulkier than the other. "She ain't gonna botha' you and you ain't gonna botha' her and I bet not eva' have to come back to these showers to get her. Are we clear on that?"

"Yeah, Ms. Dot, we clear. We didn't know she was your cellie," said the taller of the two girls.

"Ok, that's what I wanted to hear. Come on, Ava."

"Them bulldaggers won't be bothering you again. Somebody always gotta get them booty rubbing wenches togetha." They laughed as they walked back to their cell.

* * *

"Ms. Dot, you know all this time I've been in here with you, we've never talked about why you're here." Ava inquired while playing an early Saturday morning game of spades. "I know you know about my case because it was all on TV, but we have never talked about why you're in here."

Dot laid the cards on the black crate that sat between them and leaned against her bunk. "I was wondering how long it was gonna take you to ask me," Ms. Dot said with a sideways smile. "I thought maybe you was too scared to find out. Sit back and get comfortable."

By the end of her story, Ms. Dot's tears were flowing, trickling down her cheeks, chin, and onto her shirt. She told the story of how she killed her husband in a domestic dispute. She talked about her daughter, Leilani.

Ava used the bottom of her own orange shirt to wipe her own tears away and took a deep breath. Ms. Dot climbed into her bunk facing the wall, quietly weeping. Ava let her be.

* * *

Ava thought of Ms. Dot's daughter and wondered if anyone found her to inform her of her passing.

She laid down on the bed facing the wall, pulling her knees to her stomach and held the letter as close to her chest she could. After a few minutes, she opened the letter and read it.

Dear Ava,

I hope you can read this letter because you know I can't write so good, since you not here to help me. You know I won't be here much longer and by the time you get this letter I might already be dead. What a crappy way for my life to end, I'm in jail dying from cancer, no one with me, but this jail house chaplain. I just wanted to tell you baby, one mo' time before I leave this earth, to let go of yo' past. I wish I had got the chance to see my baby girl one more time before I die. Thank God every day that you had another chance to live and breathe outside these walls. Thank God that you don't have to die in here like me and so many others. I know what those boys and that girl tried to do to you hurt you real bad, but you got through it. I know it led you to doing some things that got you locked up in here.

Ms. Ava you are strong and you got a lot to live for. Don't live the rest of your life mad and bitter and holding on to the past, because if you don't let the past go, you will never know what the almighty God got for you in the future.

I love you and if I never see you again I want you to make Ms. Dot proud of you. And never forget baby, to let yo'self be blessed.

Love yo', jail Mama, Ms. Dot

Ava wept, thinking of Ms. Dot taking her last breaths in a prison hospital bed. So many questions whirled in her mind.

Was there a funeral or any type of service? Would she be buried in the potter's field along with other inmates that died and had no family and no one to claim their bodies? Would anyone in her family be contacted?

Ava made a mental note to have Sylvia check on that for her. If she was buried in the potter's field cemetery, she would make sure to have her grave marked with flowers and something other than the two wooden sticks nailed together, with a metal plate with her name and birthday on it. Ms. Dot deserved more than a jailhouse gravesite. So much more.

Receiving the news that Ms. Dot was dead shook her to her core. Ava sat up and tried to prepare herself again to get ready for the day ahead. She wanted a hug, and there was only one person who made her feel like everything would be alright with one touch. Maybe she needed to ask for the forgiveness she was supposed to give.

I wonder what Khalil is doing?

A couple of days later, in an effort to move past what happened with Khalil, Ava followed Dr. Lumpkin's advice to go see Terri for herself. She was hoping Dr. Lumpkin was free as soon as she got back to the building; she urgently needed to speak with her.

"Come on in Ava, what's wrong? Did something happen with your parents?" Dr. Lumpkin came from behind her desk, handing Ava some tissues as she sat in the adjacent chair.

Ava tried her best to compose herself. She was tired of crying and feeling sad. Going to see Terri and finding out about Ms. Dot's passing in the same week was more than she could bare.

"I followed your advice and went to see Terri." She paused and wiped her tears. "Okay, how did it go?" Dr. Lumpkin questioned.

Ava took a deep breath so her voice could speak above the tears. "Her sister Paula was there. Do you know her family was blaming me this whole time for what happened to Terri? I was trying to help Terri. I did invite her to go with me but I didn't know it was a set up, I swear I didn't know." Ava bent over in tears, holding her face in her hands. Dr. Lumpkin got up and kneeled beside her. She let her cry for a few moments, while rubbing her back.

"How did it end, what was the end result of the conversation. Take some deep breaths."

Ava cried a few more seconds then raised her head, wiping her face with the tissue.

"It ended okay. After I explained everything, her sister said she would let her family know what happened wasn't my fault. I just didn't know they were blaming me. Terri is so messed up. The only way she can communicate is with a device. She was able to let her sister know that what I said about that night was true."

Dr. Lumpkin continued rubbing her back. "You've definitely had an eventful week." They both laughed. She looked Ava square in the face. "Look at it this way. Many of your questions about Ms. Dot and Terri have been answered this week. You have the choice now to take it from here." She stood and got Ava more tissue.

Ava took a few deep breaths and sat up straight. "I guess you're right. It's all happening so fast, I guess I just wasn't ready." They both chuckled again.

They spoke for a few more moments. "Do you think you'll be able to lead your last yoga class before you go home for the weekend." Asked Dr. Lumpkin.

"Yes, I probably need it more than they do. I'll be leaving as soon as my mom gets here."

"Sounds like a plan. Go on to your room and cry a little more if you need to. Let me know if it gets too rough and I'll cancel the class."

Ava stood to leave. She gave Sylvia a big hug. "Thank you so much. It hurt to see Terri that way, but it needed to happen. I'll see you later."

CHAPTER 31

The new year came and went in ways Ava never imagined. Her father was home, she had a new job, was in school, and was fully committed to the work of helping formerly incarcerated women return to the community as productive citizens.

Ava was most proud of her work with Zola and her growth. During her time in Dwight, there were many inmates that blamed their bad behavior and attitudes on incidents of rapes and molestation. In most cases, this made their situations worse. They were sent to the hole often and some of them had their sentences increased for repeated infractions. Zola's transformation was incredible. Once she released her pain, she began to openly talk about her anger towards her mother and her healing had begun. She was more joyful and happy about her new job and moving in with her grandmother. Zola still needed to work through issues of forgiveness with her mother, but they were on a good path and having minimal dialogue.

Ava received an award for helping create a better weekend flow, and for giving the residents space to speak of more than their past hurts and imprisonments.

The weekend came and Ava decided to ride the bus home instead of having her mother pick her up. She felt something different in the air and she wanted to embrace it.

Processing what had Eli and Vera told her about how their relationship began was the icing on the cake after finding out about Khalil. Whatever her parents' truth was, hers was that she was weary of missing him.

I have to forgive Khalil. Ava decided she had already lost precious time from her life while she was in jail. She peered up at the sun in the unseasonably warm February and smiled. With a little snow on the ground, her walk from the bus stop was pleasant as she waved to her neighbors and watched the kids riding their bikes from Christmas with glee.

Three doors away from her house, Ava observed Khalil leaning against his car holding a bouquet of flowers. She didn't know what she wanted to say or how to respond, but she felt the smile slide across her face, at the same time she noticed a smile growing on his.

"Hello, Ava." Khalil said as he strutted toward Ava.

"Hello, Khalil."

"These are for you." She reached for the arrangement of orange and white stargazer lilies with one hand and put them under her nose and inhaled.

"Thank you. These are beautiful—and my favorites."

"I know," Khalil retorted, leveling a heated gaze on Ava. "Tiger and star azer lilies." He touched her elbow, "they remind me of..."

Warmth rushed to Ava's cheeks as she took in the sparkle in Khalil's eyes.

"Can I *please* have a minute to talk to you?" Khalil asked as his gaze stayed on Ava. "It won't take long, I promise. I just need to tell you everything and if you don't want to talk to me ever again, I'll never, ever bother you. But please, let me explain about that night."

"Okay, let's go inside." Ava led the way, smiling as she entered the house, and motioned for him to enter.

Khalil hesitated. "You sure it's okay, is your father home?"

Ava chuckled. "Yes he's here and yes it's okay for you to come in"

Khalil hung up his coat as Ava removed her coat and boots. Eli and Vera sat at the dining room table playing a game of Tonk.

"Good to see you again around these parts, young blood." Eli glanced up at Khalil and back to the cards as Ava and Khalil entered the living room adjacent to the dining room.

Eli and his brothers, Malik, Fred, Hambone had a meeting with Khalil one morning at the diner he frequents for breakfast after his workouts. When the discussion ended, Eli was clear that Khalil had no involvement in the attempted rape of Ava or Terri. He had discussed the situation with Ava, letting her know all was well from where he stood and it was her decision of how she wanted to move forward with Khalil.

"How are you, Khalil?" Vera asked. "You're a sight for sore eyes. Have a seat on the couch and I'll bring y'all some lemonade. Eli, don't switch these cards around when I get up." The four of them laughed.

Khalil breathed a sigh of relief as he sat on the couch. Ava sat an arm's length away from him, crossing her legs in the lotus pose.

"I've missed you, Ava," Khalil confessed. "I want you to know what was going through my head that night." Ava bowed her head, listening for the sincerity in his words. "I was on the campus for the weekend doing some research. I met Monty in the store that was near the school's campus. Monty and I had hit each other up by text and he invited me to come to a kickback at his house." Khalil sipped from the glass Vera had brought from the kitchen. Ava put her legs down, crossing her ankles.

"That night, I had no idea what his plan was. I wasn't thinking anything evil or diabolical, and I certainly wasn't thinking that he'd try to rape anybody."

Ava's glance met Khalil's eyes—she believed you could find the truth in someone's eyes. She always thought he had honest eyes and now was no different.

"Penny and I left to go to the store in my car to get more drinks and me a t-shirt. By the time we got back, an ambulance and police cars were on the scene at Monty's house. I wanted to get out and see what was happening. Penny said we should keep going and find out what happened later. I saw you walking around in a daze, and I told Penny we should take you to the hospital, but she didn't want to." Ava's eyes stung with hot tears as he continued. "I didn't understand until later that she was in on it."

Ava's heart raced as she wiped wayward tears with the back of her hand, listening to the details of the story.

"I told her I couldn't leave you walking around like that. She got out the car and just left, just like that." Khalil shifted on the couch, turning toward Ava and using one of his hands to wipe the tears that continued to moisten her cheek. "I took you to the hospital and left you because I was scared. I didn't know what to do or who to talk to. I never forgot about you, Ava. I couldn't believe it when we got the envelope about your case at the HUB."

Khalil sat the glass down and moved closer to her, taking both her hands in his. "I swear to you, I really thought it was a get-together or kickback as he called it, and that's it. I was never there to hurt you or anyone else. You saw my scar when I pulled up my shirt after I spilled the juice on myself."

"Why didn't you come forward after you found out what happened?" Ava asked, holding his gaze. "Even after taking me to the emergency room. You were able to figure it out and you were there. You could've been a witness and told everything when it happened."

"I wanted to, but my mother told me to stay out of it and finish school. My father had passed away and then my brother. She was scared for me to get involved." ".When my brother, Ali, died our family was in an uproar. There was so much going on and I needed to be there for my mother."

Ava sighed. She wanted to stay mad at him, but missing him at the same time was overwhelming. She wondered what took place when the brothers and Eli met with Khalil, and quickly let go of the thought. Although she was an adult and the decision was hers, she trusted her father's assurance, that it was okay to move forward with Khalil.

"Please forgive me," Khalil pleaded as his grin grew wider. The corners of Ava's lips turned up as her heartbeat took an uptick. "It had to be fate when Mr. Hinton sent the information to the HUB and Bernie assigned it to me. I finally admitted to Bernie that I knew about the case and my involvement."

"What did he say?" Ava inquired as her eyes widened.

"That's a story for another day. I'm here to discuss us." Khalil caressed Ava's hands. "I'm so relieved to get it out and not have that secret keep eating away at me. I quit the HUB and have my own firm, but I don't want to discuss any of that right now. Enough of all that. What about us, Ava? Will you give me another chance? I miss you so much. I miss your laugh, our talks, having lunch and dinner together. I miss us working out together and our walks in the park."

She tried to say something, but the words wouldn't come out. He gently caressed her cheek.

"I need you to forgive me, please. If you never want to see me again, I understand, but I had to tell you face to face that I never planned to hurt you or anyone. It was really a case of me being somewhere I shouldn't have been. I know I should've come forward years ago."

Ava's gaze fell to the floor, never letting go of his hands.

"We've done so much together, and we've learned a lot about each other and ourselves. I worked my ass to make sure you got out of prison. I wasn't going to stop until you were free. I knew I had only one chance to make it right. I didn't know if I was ever going to tell you, I just knew I had to give it one hundred percent and then some to right the wrong that had been done to you. I'm not willing to just throw us away. If you don't want us, bu-" this time she put her index finger to his lips.

A wave of emotion washed over her and brought quiet tears of cleansing with it. He moved over, wrapping her in his arms, and she melted against his chest, breathing in his cologne, once again, giving her permission to breathe. She didn't want to give up the relationship they were building.

"I've missed you too. Thank you so much for being honest. It's crazy how something like this could happen."

Khalil tilted her chin and gazed into her eyes. "Ava Penwood, may I have your forgiveness?"

"Yes, I forgive you."

Khalil placed a soft kiss on Ava's lips, lacing his fingers deep between her natural coils.

Eli and Vera clapped from the kitchen.

"It's about time," Vera yelled as they all laughed.

"Let's start over fresh. Right here, right now." Khalil stood and smoothed his hands over his slacks and dress shirt. "Hello, Ava. My name is Khalil, would you like to have lunch with me tomorrow?" Ava's smile spread wider with each word he spoke.

"I do believe so, Khalil," Ava replied. "What time would you like for me to be ready?"

"How about eleven-ish. Let's make it brunch. What do you say about the deli where we had our first lunch date? Ms. Shirley has been asking about you."

"It's a date." Ava gave Khalil a peck on the lips.

"I'll pick you up at eleven-thirty." Khalil stood to leave and said goodbyes to her parents on his way to the door.

"I'll see you tomorrow." He gently pulled her to him by her waist and kissed her forehead.

"Looking forward to it." She stood at the screen, watching him until he drove away. She felt like she was floating on cloud nine as she returned to the couch, waving to her parents as she went pass the dining room.

She dug her feet deep into the pillows of the sofa and snuggled a pillow under her chin and thought of Ms. Dot's last words to her.

"Don't forget to let ya' self be blessed."

She imagined her smiling face on the day she said her last goodbye "You are right about it Ms. Dot; I will let myself be blessed."

Bridgett McGill is the award-winning author of *How Does Your Garden Grow? Cultivating a Life of Abundance*, released in 2017. This inspirational book has an accompanying Interactive Journal. She released, *Birthing Purpose: 21-Day Devotional Journal* Summer of 2021 and founded the online group - Birthing Purpose. Her latest works include *The Oil: 21-Day Devotional Journal* and her first short story *Concrete Bayou*.

She is the President and Founder of the Queen Within. An organization she created to ensure women are living the best versions of themselves on a daily basis.

Bridgett is an Elementary Education teacher. She is also a certified yoga instructor with ACT yoga and practices daily to clear her mind and increase her creative flow.

Affectionately known as Ms. Bridgett, she lives in Chicago. She is the mother of two adult daughters and two grandchildren.

Visit her on the web
www.thequeenwithin.org

Also by Bridgett McGill

How Does Your Garden Grow, Cultivating a Life of Abundance
How Does Your Garden Grow, Cultivating a Life of Abundance. The Interactive Journal
Birthing Purpose: 21 - Day Devotional Journal
The Oil: 21 - Day Devotional Journal - releasing Spring 2022
Concrete Bayou releasing Summer 2022

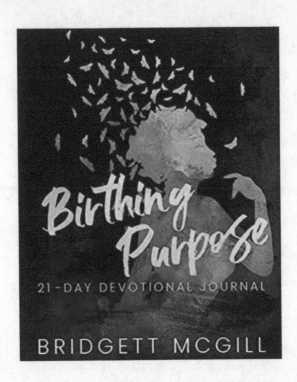

Mark Twain said *"The two most important days in your life are the day you are born and the day you find out why."*

How long have you been asking yourself the question "What is my purpose on this earth?" How long have you been trying to connect the dots and fill in the blanks? This journal is for every Beautiful and Divinely created WOMAN, who is gifted at birth with her purpose. No matter how long it takes her to see it, believe it and birth it, what she has inside her to bring forth is hers.

In the same way we can be pregnant physically, we can also be pregnant spiritually; with ideas, visions, inventions, projects, plans and the like.

Give yourself permission and be intentional in seeking your purpose. For 21 - days, allow yourself to explore hidden desires, tucked away dreams and plans unfulfilled. Don't be surprised at what you find within yourself; it's been there all the time. Get ready to walk in your purpose; the world is waiting for you.

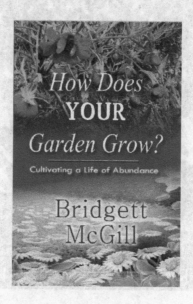

"If you compared your life to a garden right now, right today, what would you find? Is it flourishing, lush and full; are there a few green spots here and some brown patches there, or is it depleted because you've given everything away? We have to ask ourselves every day: What does my garden need? Does it need the sun of encouragement; could it benefit from the fertilizer of forgiveness; would the pruning of confession bring great relief, or is it simply craving the beauty of rest? As we walk through the gardens of our lives, we will find that we have within us, all we need to cultivate a life of abundance; we only have to be still, listen and let the beauty come forth."

CPSIA information can be obtained
at www.ICGtesting.com
Printed in the USA
BVHW081109150223
658525BV00003B/123

9 781736 783016